THE
ICEBERG
HERMIT

Arthur Roth

SCHOLASTIC INC.
New York Toronto London Auckland Sydney

With thanks to David Rattray for his editorial help,
and to Miss Elizabeth Noble and Mrs. Marion
Beeton, of the Aberdeen Public
Library, whose help
proved invaluable in
digging out the
original
story.

ISBN 0-590-44112-4

36 35 34 33 32 31 30 29 28   6 7 8/0

For Jackie, Frank, Mike, and Alexander

1

"Masthead there! Look sharp, blast yeer eyes!" the captain roared. High on the lookout point on the main mast, seventeen yearold Allan Gordon steadied himself and looked down. The captain and the first mate, two black dots far below on deck, were looking up at him. Allan watched the captain turn to the first mate and say something. Then angry voices rose again on the still cold air.

All around him Allan could hear ice scraping against the wooden sides of the *Anne Forbes*. He blew into his mittens, trying to warm his hands. The fog seemed to get inside his clothes, making him shiver. He put his hand into the pocket of his jacket and felt the small Bible his mother had given him when he left home. She had made him promise to read a page every day. So far he had only missed once, the day they had caught their first whale. In all the excitement he had forgotten his promise, but he had read two pages the next day to make up for it.

Allan had long ago decided that Captain Hughes was a liar and a bully. He shouted at everyone on the ship. Only Big Tom, the first mate, would stand up to him. But the other men, and Allan too, kept quiet when the captain began to rant and rave. Captain Hughes was the sort of man who was looking for any excuse to place a sailor in irons for mutiny. That way the captain and the shipowners would have one less share to pay out when the ship reached Aberdeen, its home port in Scotland. This was the year 1757, when sailors led a very hard life on their ships at sea.

Allan peered ahead into the whitish mist. These were iceberg seas, and he had to keep a sharp lookout. Now and again he would catch an angry word from far below as the captain and mate continued their argument.

The captain's bullying voice made Allan think of "Crab" McAfee, an old retired sailor who used to spend hours talking to Allan about life in the British Royal Navy. Crab had gone in the Royal Navy when he was only twelve. Once Crab told Allan about the bullying midshipman on one of the men-of-war who used to stand on the yardarm and stamp on the fingers of young boys as they climbed to his level. One day the midshipman fell, and his fall was seen by a dozen boys aloft in the rigging. They swung their hats and cheered the body all the way down to the deck. The doomed midshipman hit with such force that his leg bones were driven up into his body. For a moment Allan imagined the short squat body of Captain Hughes falling from the main mast, turning over and over in the air before it hit the deck. It was one way to get rid of a hated sea captain, but unfortunately Captain Hughes never climbed up into the rigging.

Through the still and windless air Allan heard the two men arguing below him.

"I don't like this fog rolling in," the captain shouted.

"Aye, we're paying now for your stubbornness," Big Tom answered.

"Oh we'll come out of it," the captain said. "I've sailed through worse than this."

"It's late in the season and we're still far to the north. We should have come about a week ago."

The captain said nothing. For the past week the first mate had been insisting that they begin the long voyage home to Scotland. Their whaling ship, the *Anne Forbes*, had spent the summer between the north of Greenland and Spitsbergen, along the edge of the polar icecap, chasing whales. Early in the season the ship had fallen in with a large school of whales that the captain had followed to the north, sailing ever deeper into the Arctic seas. Big Tom, an experienced whaler, kept urging the captain to turn about. He had never seen the sea that clear of ice so far to the north before, and he knew how suddenly treacherous the polar seas could become. Many a whaling ship had been caught in the ice and never heard of again.

But Captain Hughes was a stubborn man, and a greedy man, and he kept sailing north until the holds were almost full. Then one day, just after the whaleboat crew had lashed yet another whale to the ship's side, the captain suddenly grew alarmed. He ordered the fires under the try-pots put out and the huge iron kettles lashed down. It was time to run for home. The last whale was hauled up on deck, and for the next day or two, as the *Anne Forbes* was underway, the men cut the whale up into chunks of blubber that were packed away into barrels. The blubber from that last whale could always be melted down when the ship reached port.

But several days after hoisting sail, the *Anne Forbes* caught a northward current and made very little headway. Even worse, the polar seas were beginning to freeze over. Soon the vessel was surrounded by bobbing ice floes that every day grew more thick and numerous.

To add to their troubles, a heavy fog lay over the water. The mate guessed that the fog meant the nearby presence of an iceberg or large ice field. He had seen those Arctic fogs before. He knew too that whaling ships were sometimes trapped in the ice all winter, and when that happened the crews of such ships usually died from the cold, or from hunger, or from the dread sickness known as scurvy. And those were slow and painful ways to die, with none of the swift mercy of drowning.

Now the ice floes were closing in on all sides of the *Anne Forbes*. Even Allan Gordon, high up on his lookout platform on the main mast, could hear the scrape of ice against the wooden sides of the vessel. Allan peered into the fog. On all sides he could spot cakes of ice bobbing past. As far as he could see the water was dotted with ice floes of all shapes and sizes. Several times he spotted a large ice island, where dozens of floes had frozen to each other. But Allan was not worried. This was his first whaling trip into the northern seas and he did not realize the danger. High up on the mast he thought only of his return home. With fair sailing weather they could make it back to Scotland in a couple of weeks. It had been a good voyage, their holds were full, and Allan would make more money from this one trip than he had in three years of fishing. His mother would be pleased. Allan's father was dead, and they needed the money at home. He would also be able to buy a nice present for his girlfriend, Nancy.

Despite the cold and fog and ice, Allan was happy to be a whaler. He was in excellent health, making good money at an adventurous job, and he had already traveled more and seen more sights than most people did in a lifetime. What seventeen-year-old lad could ask for more?

Allan had signed on the *Anne Forbes* four months before, entitled to a full seaman's share of the profits from the voyage. In those days a seaman could make more money from whaling than any other kind of sea duty. The work was hard and dangerous, but it paid very well. Whale oil was in great demand. Before the discovery of crude oil, people burned whale oil in their lamps. Whalebone was used in ladies' garments, while perfume and cosmetics were made from other parts of the whale. Although Allan was only seventeen, he had already worked three years on fishing ships in his home port of Aberdeen. In those days it was common for twelve-, thirteen-, and fourteen-year-old boys to go to sea.

Allan had worked twelve hours a day, six days a week, for a tailor in Scotland, before he went to sea. So he was well used to hard work. He was a strong, well-built youth who stood five feet nine inches tall, and weighed 160 pounds. He had blue eyes and straw-colored hair and a tiny cleft in the point of his chin.

Around Allan the canvas sails flapped lazily in the odd breeze the ship caught. As usual with fog, there was little wind and the ship was making slow headway. Suddenly Allan came alert. For a moment he thought he spotted land ahead. He knew the *Anne Forbes* was not far from the north Greenland coast and it was possible that an uncharted island lay in the vessel's path. He lowered his head and narrowed his eyes as he tried to peer through the fog. But he could make out nothing. The afternoon light was failing and it was hard to see ahead for any distance.

But there! Now it loomed in front of him, a solid greenish-white wall of ice. He turned and shouted down with all his might.

"Berg! Dead ahead! Berg! Dead ahead!"

Down below Captain Hughes yelled a command to the helmsman. "Hard a port, blast yeer clumsy claws! Hard a port! Port! PORT!" The *Anne Forbes* slowly began a turn to port.

But it was too late. The ship hit the ice almost head on, a heavy smashing blow. Both mate and captain were thrown to the deck. The crash whipped the top of the mast forward like the tip of a fishing rod and Allan flew from his lookout post. He hit a sail below and clutched at it desperately, but his mittened fingers could not get a grip. He half slid, half fell, down the sail until he hit a spar. The blow knocked the breath from him but he had sense enough to hook one arm under a rope and hang on.

After several moments of just hanging there, he managed to pull himself up and onto the yardarm. Then he looked down. Spars were snapping off with such fury that they sounded like gunshots. Sails hung sideways, all fouled in the rigging. Already one mast had crashed on to the deck. Allan picked his way to the very end of the yardarm. There, some twenty feet below was the flat surface of a ledge on the iceberg. Between the wreckage of the crippled ship and the smooth hard surface of the ice, Allan chose the ice and dropped from the end of the yardarm. This time the force of the fall knocked him out.

On board the *Anne Forbes* all was confusion. The ice wall against which the ship was pinned gave no foothold to anyone. The ship had started to sink, and an attempt was being made to lower one of the whaleboats on the sea side of the vessel. The whaleboat no sooner reached the water when a large ice floe smashed it to pieces against the side of the

Anne Forbes. Bodies spilled into the sea. Other ice floes began to build against the seaward side of the ship. As the *Anne Forbes* settled lower in the water, large blocks of ice rode in over the side, forcing the vessel to list even more until the seawater came pouring in over her gunwales.

All the sailors were now up on deck, desperately trying to save themselves. Some threw hatchcovers into the sea and jumped in after them, hoping to use them as rafts. Quite a few had climbed the rigging, but with the tilt of the ship to seaward, they had no hope of reaching the top of the ice wall and were now simply hanging on to ropes and spars.

Captain Hughes had gone down to his cabin to snatch up the ship's log and other valuable papers. Big Tom, bracing himself against the slope of the deck, looked around at all the others. There was a slight smile on his face. The desperate efforts, the panic, the scurrying to and fro, the captain trying to save the log, all of this seemed senseless to the mate. For he knew too much, knew they were all doomed, knew that the men who had jumped overboard would only last minutes in the freezing water, knew it was only a matter of time before the Arctic claimed another fifty victims. He looked up in the rigging, wondering what had happened to Allan Gordon. He felt a wave of pity for the seventeen-year-old-youth out on his first voyage. Allan was nowhere to be seen and the mate decided that he must have been thrown into the water and was no doubt drowned by now.

"Get it over with," Big Tom muttered to himself, then ran down the sloping deck and dived cleanly over the rail to his death in the icy waters.

Above on the ice field Allan Gordon groaned, then forced himself to sit up. He was just in time to see the top of the ship's mast disappear from sight. The *Anne Forbes* had gone down in minutes, with all hands, and Allan was alone on a field of ice, somewhere off the coast of Greenland, with no food, no water and no hope of rescue.

Allan looked around. Nearby there were some dim white shapes that he knew to be ice boulders but they were the only things to be seen. Everywhere he looked there was fog and ice and piercing cold. He felt a desperate loneliness, as though he were the only person in the whole world. Without food, without water, with no way of keeping warm, he was doomed. Death would come in a matter of days, perhaps even hours.

It was so unfair, he thought. In one moment he was a happy young man on his way home to his family and girlfriend with plenty of money honestly earned, and in the next minute he was sitting all alone on a piece of ice in the middle of the Arctic seas, waiting for death to come.

He got to his feet, staggered over to one of the ice boulders and sank down behind it, trying to find some shelter from the cold. He wrapped his arms around his sides, hugging himself, and began to sway back and forth. "I'm going to die," he said aloud. "I'm going to die right here, all alone, and no one will ever know about it."

He thought then of his mother and of his three younger sisters: Jean, Flora, and Gladys. They would wait for word of the *Anne Forbes* and as the months and then the years passed, they would learn to accept the fact that Allan was dead. And wee "Bunty" Duff would finally be right about Allan. However, if the schoolmaster were right, then the old fortuneteller had to be wrong.

Thinking of his mother, Allan reached a hand into his pocket and took out the Bible. There was just enough light to read his daily page.

When he was finished reading, he carefully marked his place in the Bible with a thin, flat piece of whalebone that he used as a bookmark, then put the book away in his pocket and thought that in his present situation saying a prayer was about the only possible way he could help himself.

But he had little faith that prayer would save him either. Squinching down into his clothes as much as possible to keep warm, he sat there and waited for the end.

2

No matter how he tried, Allan could not sleep longer than a few minutes at a time. If it was not one thing, it was another. The noise of a piece of drift ice smashing into the side of the ice field would jolt him awake and leave him trembling with fear. Or his feet would get too cold and start to throb with pain. Or the heat of his body would melt the ice he was sitting on, and the melted icewater would soak into his pants and force him to move to a new place.

He thought the night would never end, though he realized that the coming of daylight would hardly improve matters. Again and again during the night he went over his situation and each time found it hopeless. He discovered that the ice around him was frozen seawater and not fit to drink. As for food, even if a seal or some seabirds came to the ice field, he had no way of killing them. And if by

13

some miracle he found food and water, without fire he could not last very long in the bitter cold of the Arctic winter. He had survived drowning only to die from starvation and exposure.

There was only one very slim chance of rescue, that within the next day or two a passing ship might spot him and take him off his ice island. But the *Anne Forbes* had been late in turning about for home, and all the other whaling ships had no doubt left the polar seas by now. And even if one of the whalers were still in the area, the chances of that particular ship sailing close enough to the ice field to see him were one in a million.

The dawn came and Allan stirred himself. The fog had finally lifted, a day too late for the *Anne Forbes*. He stood up and looked out over the frozen ice field. The first thing he noticed was a tall mountain of ice some hundred yards away. Looking at that ice peak, he felt the first stirring of hope. It was obviously an iceberg, and icebergs he knew were originally made of frozen snow and therefore had no salt. With freshwater from an iceberg, he could survive for eight to ten days, perhaps even two weeks. During the night he had tasted a chip of ice and found it salty. But now he guessed that the unbroken ice field that stretched away as far as he could see was made of frozen seawater that had trapped the freshwater iceberg in its grip, like a raisin on the surface of a cake.

Allan turned slowly around until he was looking at the spot where the *Anne Forbes* went down. Then he rubbed his eyes and looked again. It was still there — a long, rounded black hump frozen into the ice. Surely it was the carcass of a huge dead whale that had somehow broken loose from another whaler and drifted until it froze into the edge of the ice field.

A miracle, Allan thought, as he ran and stumbled over the ice. Suddenly he had a mountain of freshwater and more food than he could eat in a year. When he reached the scene, he found an even greater miracle than he had dared to hope for. What he thought was a whale carcass turned out to be the black upturned bottom of a ship. After the shock wore off, Allan realized that the ship had to be the *Anne Forbes*. He could hardly believe his good luck! A moment ago he had neither food, water, nor shelter. Now he had all three.

With some difficulty Allan made his way over to the *Anne Forbes*. Everywhere the ice was all jumbled up and hard to climb over. He found a broken piece of spar that had been thrown onto the ice when the ship went down, and used it as a staff to help him over the rough places. Finally he reached the keel of the vessel only to be frustrated again. How was he to get inside the *Anne Forbes*? The keel and bottom of the ship was made of thick oak and he had nothing that would cut a hole through the tough wood. He was in danger of starving to death with a ship full of food only a few feet away.

Then he remembered the captain's cabin at the rear of the vessel, a cabin with a small window that he might be able to squeeze through! If he could dig down through the ice and reach that window, he could crawl through and into the cabin. Once inside the captain's cabin he would have shelter, and surely he would find some food. But how could he reach the cabin with nothing to break or chop with?

By now Allan had a raging thirst. His last drink of water had been the day before, and the piece of salt ice he had sucked on during the night had only added to his thirst. Before he could attempt to get into the *Anne Forbes*, he would have to hike over to the ice mountain. Even if he got inside the ship right away, it would not help him. Any of the water that was stored aboard in barrels would now be mixed with seawater and not fit to drink.

Allan turned around and headed for the iceberg peak. Again it was very slow going over the humped-up blocks and piles of ice, and he often had to stop for a rest. It took him over an hour but he finally made it to the foot of the mountain. He knocked a chip of ice loose with his staff and found, to his great joy, that the ice was free of salt. He drank until he was satisfied, knocking pieces loose and letting them melt in his mouth. After that he remembered his promise to his mother, took out the Bible, and read a page.

Allan looked up at the towering peak of ice above him. If there were only some way he could cut steps to the top of that mountain, he could see for miles. He could even put up a signal of some kind, a flag that might be noticed by a passing ship. At the moment, however, he had to return to the *Anne Forbes* and figure out some way of getting inside the ship. He knocked loose a large chunk of ice and jammed it into the pocket of his jacket so that he would have something to drink later on.

This time Allan took what he hoped would be an easier way back to the *Anne Forbes*. Making his way through and over the jumbled ice, he had to take frequent detours to avoid knee-deep pools of slush, or ice ridges that were too high or too difficult to climb. He had almost reached the ship when he spotted a pile of smashed timbers off to one side. He went over to investigate and found the remains of an open whaleboat that had been stored on the deck of the *Anne Forbes*. The whaleboat had somehow been thrown clear at the time of the collision. Although it was smashed beyond repair, what excited Allan was finding several articles tangled up in the wreck.

He pulled out a couple of pieces of sailcloth, a coil of rope, an iron harpoon head, and the whaleboat's anchor. The anchor was shaped like the head of a pick, and he lifted it up in his hands, raised it above his head and let one of the points come down on the ice. He grunted with satisfaction. It wouldn't be the easiest tool in the world to work with, but between it and the harpoon head he ought to be able to chip away at the ice surrounding the *Anne Forbes*.

Later, after half an hour's work, he stopped to rest for a moment. He figured that the captain's window was somewhere between six and ten feet below the surface of the ice. Which meant that he could not dig straight down, or he might not be able to climb back up and out of the hole again. He would have to start well back and dig an open trench that sloped down to the window.

He still had trouble believing his good luck. During the night the sunken ship had somehow turned turtle and been forced to surface again. Perhaps the air trapped in the holds was responsible. But the miracle would do him no good if he could not get inside the vessel. He jumped to his feet and went back to hacking at the ice. Several times he was tempted to give up digging. Even if he got into the ship, it did not mean that he was saved. Any food on the *Anne Forbes* would have been spoiled by seawater. He might live a week or two longer inside the ship, but in the long run he was doomed. But what finally stopped him from giving up was the memory of Bunty Duff talking to his mother that soft spring morning over five years ago. Thinking of Bunty made Allan tighten his lips and go back to smashing at the ice. Thinking of Bunty could have made him mad enough to do anything.

When dark came he still had not reached the captain's window. He spread a piece of sailcloth on the bottom of the trench, lay down and rested his head on the coil of rope, then pulled another piece of sailcloth over his face. Hoping to keep warm, he pretended he was sitting on his favorite stool in front of the fire at his home in Aberdeen. He thought he heard his mother say, "Allan, it's time to go to bed." She would lift the oil lamp down from the wall and wait until he climbed the ladder to the sleeping loft above the kitchen.

There he would lie face down on his straw mattress and look into the kitchen through the wide crack between the floorboards. He would watch his mother tilt her hand above the chimney globe of the lamp. A quick puff of breath and the flame would go out, leaving everything in darkness. Then he would turn over, link his hands beneath his head and listen to the soft pitter-patter of rain on the thatched roof.

And listening to the rain, he finally fell asleep.

3

Allan passed another miserable night, though it wasn't quite as bad as the night before. Lying on the bottom of the trench and sheltered from the wind, he was able to catch catnaps of half an hour or so before the cold got through to his feet, or the hard ice he was lying on proved too uncomfortable. Then he would sit up, rearrange his canvas blankets and try to fold his body in such a way as to get warm and comfortable again.

When dawn finally woke him for the last time, he got to his feet and folded and set aside the two pieces of sailcloth. Then he began swinging his arms around his body to get warm. After that he was ready to start hacking at the ice again. He had to get into that cabin. So far the weather had not been too cold, but if a bad storm came along, with freezing temperatures, he might not be able to survive another night without shelter of some kind.

His third or fourth awkward blow with the anchor tip hit a piece of framing wood around the captain's window. Allan set aside the anchor, took up the lance and jabbed away until he had uncovered the top of the window. He had been afraid that the window would be too small to crawl through. If that happened, then he had no tools that could cut the tough oak planks of the ship's stern and enlarge the window frame. But fortunately the window was large enough to crawl through easily.

Another half hour of hard work and he had cleared the ice away from the rest of the window. He broke out all the glass with the lance, then crawled through. Once inside the cabin he had to wait for a few minutes until his eyes got used to the darkness.

Since the ship was upside down, Allan was now walking on the cabin ceiling. When he recovered his eyesight, he saw that everything on the floor of the cabin lay strewn on the ceiling. Allan picked his way over the jumbled mass of clothing and papers and dishes and found the captain's private bread locker. Inside the locker there were several large tin boxes. He dragged one out, turned it right side up, and lifted the lid. The box was jammed full of special biscuits that the captain was particularly fond of. Allan grabbed a handful, found a chair and set it on its legs, then sat down to enjoy his first bite of food in almost two days. He bit into a biscuit, crammed it into his mouth, then groaned with pleasure. He had never eaten anything that tasted so good. Slowly, enjoying every bite, he ate about two dozen of the biscuits and blessed old Captain Hughes for having a sweet tooth.

One thing that surprised Allan was that the biscuits were dry. He opened two more of the tin boxes, and they too were dry inside. As he explored the cabin, he found that although many things, especially clothes, were wet, other articles in boxes and closets were dry. Which meant that the ship could not have been underwater very long, perhaps only ten minutes or so. It was almost dark when the ship went down so that Allan could not know when the *Anne Forbes* came to the surface again. The ship, turned turtle, must have been there on the edge of the ice all night, although Allan did not find the upturned keel until morning.

Much later Allan discovered that the ship had been turned over and forced to the surface by a sloping underwater ledge of ice that acted like a ramp or shovel. The ice field was drifting north with the current and the *Anne Forbes*, caught between the force of the ice field and the opposing ice floes, had swiftly been worked to the surface.

The biscuits made Allan thirsty again and

he searched through the cabin for something to drink. He came across a locked cabinet and forced it open with the harpoon head. Inside he found a jumble of broken and empty bottles. Lying on top of all the broken glass was a barrel full of some liquid. He picked through the knives and forks that were scattered over the floor, looking for something that would make a hole. He finally found a corkscrew and with it drilled through the top of the barrel. Then he lifted the barrel on to the chair, tilted it over on its side and spilled some of the liquid into a pewter mug that he had picked up from the floor.

He took a drink of the brownish liquid and nearly choked. It was either brandy or rum. He was not used to the taste of alcohol and could not tell the difference. He didn't like the taste but he managed to get down several long swallows of the stuff for he knew that the liquor would soon warm him up inside.

Then Allan went sorting through the stuff in the captain's cabin and found many useful articles, including a large carving knife. He'd hoped to locate the captain's spyglass but he could not find it anywhere. Perhaps the captain had it with him up on deck when the ship struck the iceberg. If so, the telescope was no doubt lost. He did find a boathook and the captain's speaking trumpet, a sort of hand-held loudspeaker. He also found many of the captain's clothes. They were nearly all wet, and were half frozen, but Allan knew that he would find a use for everything later on.

After a while the strong drink took effect and he began to feel drowsy. He had slept little the night before and he was exhausted after his hiking over the rough ice and his hours in digging the tunnel to the cabin window.

He dragged the captain's mattress into the large clothes closet and piled all the clothes he could find on top of it. The mattress and the clothes were fairly wet, but he did manage to find a few coats and jackets that were halfway dry and these he piled on top of himself. Then he shut the door of the closet. There was very little space left, but that was a good thing, he knew. The heat of his body would warm the air trapped in the closet and help hold back the cold air outside.

Although he was quite tired, Allan did not go to sleep right away. He actually felt somewhat happy. A sort of miracle had happened. He had shelter, and enough food and water to last for a couple of weeks.

Lying there in the clothes closet Allan thought of his girlfriend Nancy and began to sing "Annie Laurie." an old Scottish love song. He finished the song and laughed out loud. He was somewhat drunk, so he was. Allan Gordon, of 16 Keith Street, Aberdeen, wished to inform the present company that he felt rather jolly. But he would have to find fire if he wanted to last through the whole winter. Well so he would. He would have lovely big warm fires for there was coal on board. There were also a couple of stoves on the *Anne Forbes*, and he would find them too.

And he might as well elect himself captain, he thought. If he had to look after the whole ship by himself, then he ought to be at least a captain. "Captain Gordon," he said aloud. "Did you hear that, master? Wee stupid Allan is now a captain." He laughed again.

"Jump to it, blast ye!" he roared inside the closet. "When Captain Gordon gives an order, he wants to see nothing but heels flashing up the rigging."

But as quickly as his happiness came, it went away again, and soon he felt very sorry for himself. He was all alone in the Arctic seas, the nearest person a thousand miles away, and there wasn't a soul in the world who knew of his existence. He might as well be dead, for wasn't he already in an icy grave? And he had as little chance of getting out of this grave as he had of getting out of a real grave in the earth.

For some reason then he thought of the

fortuneteller whose tent he went into the day of the last Autumn Hiring Fair in Aberdeen. At the time he was sixteen and had been working as a deckhand on the fishing trawler *Queen of Argyle*. He sat on a stool inside the dimly lit tent and gave the old gypsy woman a silver threepenny piece. She lifted his right hand to the top of a small table and began to study it. She felt the hard skin on his palms and noticed the half dozen scars where fish-cleaning knives had nicked his fingers. "You're a lad that works with your hands. You're not a fancy clerk or scholar."

"I work on a fishing boat."

"Aye, I thought so." The old woman traced a long line across his palm. "You're going to make a big change very soon. You'll change either your work or where you live. And then, within a space of four, you'll start out on a long voyage over deep waters."

"The water isn't shallow where I go out fishing," Allan pointed out.

"Aye, but this will be a long voyage to foreign parts, a strange voyage full of danger. You will be in great trouble. Beware of a dark man with a twisted face. But you will have friends. A very good friend, a fair lady, will save your life but will not talk to you."

"But how can that be?" Allan asked. "Will this lady friend be deaf and dumb?"

"I know not. I can only tell there will be great love but no words between you."

"And then?" Allan said.

"And then you will come home within a space of seven and you will be very rich indeed, having found a great treasure."

"Will it be gold?"

"No, not gold, but something of great value. It is hidden from me."

"And my girlfriend, what do you see of her?"

"That line is hard to read. But you will live a long time and have a merry life."

Allan asked other questions, but the old woman said she had told him enough and if he wanted more exact information on whom he was going to marry, then he would have to give her another silver coin — this time a sixpence.

"You must think I'm a great fool," Allan said and left the tent. It was all a bunch of foolishness anyway — space of four and space of seven and a fair lady over deep waters.

And now, inside the hulk of the *Anne Forbes,* he thought once again of the fortuneteller. Some things had indeed come true. He did change his job and go on a long voyage to foreign parts. And true enough it was a strange voyage full of danger. But where was the fair lady who would save his life? And how could he ever return from the voyage with a great treasure? He would be lucky indeed if he got back home with his life.

"Poor wee Allan Gordon," he said in the darkness of the closet. "Poor wee laddie, you've escaped drowning only to go mad from loneliness in an icy hulk stuck fast to an iceberg."

And because of the alcohol working on him, he began to cry and murmur, over and over again, the names of his loved ones: his mother, Nancy, his sisters Jean, Flora, and Gladys.

And still sniffling a bit, he drifted off to sleep.

4

Allan woke up early in the morning, stiff with cold and with a pounding headache. He was also dying for a drink of water. Fortunately a heavy coat of hoarfrost had formed on the inside walls of the cabin, and by chipping this off he was able to get enough moisture to satisfy his thirst.

After this first mouthful, Allan took the carving knife and scraped frost off the walls until the pewter mug was half full. Then he went over to the barrel and filled the mug to the brim with rum. He took the rum and water, sat on the chair and stared around at the cabin. He was still exhausted from his work of the day before. His arms felt as heavy as lead and it was a struggle just to lift his legs. But he had to plan things out, get everything in the cabin picked up and put away. He had to make some sort of cover for his opening to the outside, and he had to see about breaking through to the rest of the ship.

But for now it was so good to sit there and feel the rum start working its way through his body, warming his insides and his legs and arms. When he felt warm all over he went outside to answer the call of nature. The sky was overcast and it was quite cold, around the freezing mark he guessed.

He climbed up on top of the rounded back of the *Anne Forbes* and looked in all directions. The first thing he noticed was that the ship was no longer on the edge of the open water. The *Anne Forbes* was now frozen in on the seaward side by a solid fifty yards of piled up ice floes. This pleased Allan because it lessened the danger of the *Anne Forbes* breaking loose and going to the bottom.

Allan shaded his eyes and looked over the open seawater. There wasn't a hint of a sail anywhere, but then he didn't really expect to see one. He should rig up a pole and flag of some sort to use as a signal, but what was the use? There were no ships anywhere in his area.

Feeling depressed again, he climbed down from the keel and went back inside the *Anne Forbes*. He poured himself another half mug of rum and took a couple of long swallows. He might as well get drunk, what difference did it make? He was a dead man anyway. If he didn't die from starvation or thirst, then the cold would finish him off. And if he managed to survive the cold somehow, then loneliness would drive him mad.

He finished the rest of the rum, staggered over to the closet and climbed in. Shutting the door behind him, he sank down on the bedclothes and pretended he was back home in his own bed. He didn't want to think of the world outside his closet door, didn't want to face the fact that the days were getting shorter and that in a few more weeks there would be no daylight left at all — nothing but constant darkness for three months or more. And the sea would be a solid sheet of ice for hundreds of miles in all directions.

Allan shook his head. He was done for, there was no mistake about that. Even if he found enough food and water on the *Anne Forbes* to carry on a hike over the frozen ice to the nearest land, he didn't know in what direction to travel. And even if he made it to land, which would be a miracle, he was still likely to starve to death. He did not know how to hunt or find food the way the Eskimos could. Which meant that he would have to find some Eskimos and hope that they would feed him. The trouble was that Eskimos were few and far between in the polar regions. It would take another miracle to find them.

"I'm a dead man," Allan said aloud in the

darkness. "A living dead man." It would take too many miracles to save him, and he had already been granted one miracle, being the only one still alive from the shipwreck. To expect three or four miracles in a row was madness.

And if he stayed on the *Anne Forbes,* if he managed to find enough food to survive through the winter? Chances were that the ship would sink when the ice broke up in the spring. And should he manage to stay on the iceberg after spring came, the berg would drift south and eventually melt. So either way he was doomed, and no one would ever find out what had happened to Allan Gordon and the *Anne Forbes*.

Mercifully the rum went to work and Allan soon fell asleep. Hours later he woke up shivering. He fumbled his way out of the closet, scraped some ice off the wall of the cabin, and then sat down, ate a dozen biscuits, and drank a mug full of rum.

He stared blankly at the cabin window, where the daylight was already starting to fade. He should do something, there was something he had to do but he could not remember what it was. Ah, but that rum felt good. He was on the *Anne Forbes* only there was no one else with him. What happened? Where was everybody? Why was it getting dark so soon?

He stood up and then watched in amazement as his body fell to the cabin floor. Here now, that won't do at all Allan Gordon, he scolded himself. You are a regular drunken sot and a disgrace to the whole Gordon clan. Come now, like a good lad, get to your feet and climb back into bed.

Somehow he made it back to the closet and tumbled inside. It took him a good five minutes to get the door closed and his body arranged beneath the bedclothes.

He began to think of home then, and his memories carried him swiftly back. It was Saturday morning and he was a twelve-year-old lad again, with a pair of bright tin pails, picking blackberries out of the hedges lining the road that ran past his house. He filled both pails, walked down the lane, and turned in the gate to his cottage. He was walking toward the front door, about to call out to his mother, when he heard a voice he hated above all others, the voice of Bunty Duff, the schoolmaster. He tiptoed past the door, set the blackberries on top of the wooden churn in the storeroom, then went around by the back of the house and squeezed himself beneath the rear window of the kitchen. He sat with his back against the whitewashed stones of the wall and listened to the conversation that was going on inside.

"Another two years would be wasted on him," Bunty said. "He's a good size now and ready for work. He's picked up a bit of reading but he's hopeless at writing. It's all he can do to write his name. Put him to work — he hasn't the brains for school."

"Aye, right enough the lad shows no taste for the books," his mother agreed. "Still I thought it would be nice if he stayed through the sixth grade. Then he might be taken on to learn a trade or work in a nice shop."

"Ach, not that lad," the master said scornfully. "Put him to work right away, woman. He's a lazy lump and he hasn't brains enough to fill a thimble."

Allan stole away into the orchard and hugged himself with glee. Hallelujah, he was all through with school! Never again would Bunty give him six cuts of the bamboo cane across the fingertips. Never again would the master bang his head against the blackboard or keep him late after school. He was free at last! All summer he had begged his mother to let him go to work in September instead of back to school. And now his prayers were answered. Now he would wear long pants and a cloth cap and learn to whistle at girls. But happy as he was, a little poison entered his soul. He had not known that he was stupid. If the master said he was stupid then it must be so, because who could tell better than the master? But what harm if he were stupid, who wanted to go around with his head stuck in a book all the time? And if he wasn't the brightest lad in the world, he could make up for it in other ways. He was cheerful, and a hard worker, and those things were important too.

Allan groaned and sat up. Night or day? He pushed open the door of the closet. It was pitch black and piercing cold. He hurried to the rum barrel, patting his way with his hands, and poured himself another mug of the burning liquid.

A fast trip outside, then he got back into the closet and waited for the rum to stupefy his brain again and let him forget the ice and cold and loneliness. And again the rum worked and he drifted off into a strange hazy world of dreams and old memories and vague plans for the future, a dream world that ignored the silent icy waters outside the captain's cabin.

And so Allan lost track of the time. All he did was sleep and drink rum, although once in a while he would stir himself enough to eat a few biscuits or chip some ice from the cabin walls. Whenever he woke up he would drink a cup or two of rum, wait until he was nice and warm and feeling drowsy, then climb back into the closet, burrow underneath the jumbled pile of clothing, and go back to sleep.

When the cold woke him several hours later, he would drink another cup of rum and repeat the routine. It was a vicious circle. He would wake up shivering and would have to drink a sizable amount of rum to bring warmth to his body. However, the rum would soon make him sleepy and he would head back to the comfort of the closet.

It was the third or fourth day since he had broken into the ship and Allan lay in the closet, thinking of Mister Craigie, his first boss on leaving school. Allan had been apprenticed to William Craigie, a tailor in Aberdeen, and spent twelve hours every day in keeping the shop clean, in running errands, in sorting wool and worsteds, in making the long simple stitches in first-run sewing, in picking loose threads off completed coats and jackets, in scrubbing the master tailor's lapboard every morning, in waxing threads, in effect doing the hundred and one things that made Mister Craigie's life a little easier. Was that Mister Craigie shouting?

Allan slid back and forth between his dream world and the real world outside his closet. Where was he? What was going on? Someone wanted him, was calling for him. Was it the Yellow Man coming out of the orchard? But there was no one there. He was all alone on the *Anne Forbes*. Or was he back in Craigie's shop? Or were those voices in his dream? Or had someone broken into his cabin and was right now eating his biscuits? That's what it sounded like!

Hung over, half asleep, sick and confused, Allan worked the closet door open and peered out. He was just in time to see the heels and legs of a woman flash through the window! He distinctly saw the bare soles and pink toes of her rather large feet.

He tumbled out of the closet, not knowing what to expect. Picking up the boathook in one hand and a harpoon in the other, he went to the entrance he had tunneled out. There, above him on the ice, were several polar bears!

They had been drawn to the ship by the smell of blubber coming from the holds and were now trying to dig their way into the *Anne Forbes*. Allan was horrified at the size of the holes they were making in the ice with their powerful paws! But something else shocked him even more. Two of the bears had managed to drag forth several bodies, and Allan thought that one of them was the corpse of his late captain! The bodies must have been those of sailors who had been thrown into the water when the *Anne Forbes* went down. Shortly after the collision they must have floated to the top of the water and then become frozen into the new ice that was constantly forming. With fear and disgust, Allan watched the bears tear at the corpses. He had to get rid of them, chase them away from the ship. He went back inside the cabin for the captain's speaking trumpet. Carrying the trumpet outside he stopped at the end of the tunnel and shouted with all his might, "Avast, ye lubbers!"

Two bears stood up on their hind feet and stared with curiosity at Allan. The animals appeared to be eight feet tall. After a minute or so they dropped to all fours again and resumed their feeding.

The polar bears were not a bit frightened of Allan. They are the largest land animals to be found in Arctic regions, and most of them never see a human being. With the exception of the male walrus, whose tusks they fear, polar bears will attack and kill any animal they run across.

Again Allan shouted at the bears, still hoping to scare them away. Finally one of the huge beasts took an interest in Allan. Lazily the big white bear swung around and began to pad his way toward the tunnel.

Allan, his head finally clearing of sleep and confusion, suddenly realized the danger he was in. He ducked back into the cabin and looked wildly around for something to block the window. He found an iron grate that was used to barricade the window against thieves when the *Anne Forbes* was in port. He dropped the gate into its slots. But would that be enough? All that one of those powerful bears had to do was push hard with one paw and the whole grate would break away from the window frame.

For a moment Allan stood still. Then he heard the snuffling of the bear at the end of the tunnel. Allan grabbed up the lance and stuck it out between the bars of the grate. He would jab with the lance when the bear reached the window. He waited several minutes, but the bear, though still at the end of the tunnel, did not come any closer.

Allan continued to wait, his heart thumping wildly in his chest. Still the bear did not come any nearer. Allan withdrew the lance and leaned it against the wall near the window. He had a new idea. He would tie knives and forks to the grating, with their points facing outwards, so that the bear could not get close enough to the window frame.

He had earlier noted a large ball of string on the floor and picked it up, along with a half a dozen knives and forks from the captain's personal silverware. Working as quickly as he could, he tied the utensils to the bars of the grate, cursing his stiff and awkward fingers as he worked. He was so nervous and excited, so afraid that the bear would suddenly charge the window, that he kept dropping things.

And for some reason he could not get the knives and forks to stay well-tied. He would wrap a knife and plenty of cord, and then minutes later the point would be drooping as the string mysteriously lost its holding power. He forced himself to be calm and work slowly. What made everything twice as hard was the knowledge that the bear was still at the end of the tunnel. Every once in a while Allan's work would be interrupted by the sound of a grunt or a cough from the animal. Each time it happened, Allan's heart stood still and he stopped what he was doing and grabbed up a lance.

Finally, though, he had a dozen sharp-pointed knives and forks tied to the bars of the grate. Feeling a little safer, he withdrew from the window and sat down in a chair, the lance resting across his knees.

Allan soon found, to his surprise, that he was sweating. The excitement and the fear had driven all the cold from his body. It was strange how all of a sudden he wanted to live, he wanted to survive and go back to Scotland to see his family again. For a while there, for three or four days, he had not cared whether he lived or died. But out on the ice, when he realized the bear was coming for him, he had also realized that he had given up. And he had given up without a struggle. Just then, when it looked as though he might be killed, he felt a terrible wave of self-pity surge through him. Because young Allan Gordon had been given, through a miracle, the gift of continued life. And Allan Gordon, like a great big baby afraid of being left alone in the dark, had curled up and pulled the blanket over his head. He was acting just as he used to act when he was afraid of the Yellow Man, the strange unknown monster who lived at the back of the orchard when he was just a baby. For years he had feared the Yellow Man, knew that some day the Yellow Man would leave his secret cave in the orchard and come into the house and gobble him up. He was nine or ten before he got over his fear of the Yellow Man and finally realized that such a monster did not exist. And the strange thing was that Allan could no longer remember who had first told him about the Yellow Man. For years Allan had been afraid of something that no one else knew anything about, something that he must have made up himself when he was just a child. Because when Allan finally described the Yellow Man to his mother, she had never heard of such a creature before in her whole life. Instead of hands and feet, the Yellow Man had huge yellow claws, like a lobster. His nose was a long yellow trunk like an elephant's, and from the bottoms of his ears two long yellow tails hung down. Those tails could whip around your back and hold you tight while the claws tore chunks out of your flesh. There was only one good thing about the Yellow Man — because of those hard yellow claws on the ends of his legs, he could not run very fast. But if he ever cornered you, it was awful what would happen.

Allan went over to the window frame, looked out and listened. There was no sight or sound of the bear nearby although he could hear claws scraping farther out on the ice. He left the lance leaning against the window and went back to his chair. Old Bunty was right, he didn't have a thimbleful of brains or he would never have gone out on the ice and stirred up the brutes. He hadn't been thinking straight.

Allan went over to the bread locker. Some time in the past day or night he had left one of the tins of biscuits on the floor with the lid off, instead of putting it back inside the locker. The bear had pulled most of the biscuits out of the tin and scattered them over the floor. That was probably when he woke up, Allan decided. He began to pick up as many of the biscuits as he could find. At least the other two tins were safe inside the bread locker.

Allan now realized that his despair and fear

had led him into a very dangerous practice. From now on, he promised himself, he would only drink rum when it was absolutely necessary to get warm or to stay alive. He had been what the master said he was, a lazy lump with no brains. He had plenty of work to keep him busy. He had to get some order into the cabin. He had to get into the other holds and find a stove and coal and more food than just those biscuits. Even though he might never get off the iceberg alive, the least he could do was to see how long he could last before the end came.

He put the tin of biscuits away in the food locker and pulled the Bible out of his pocket. The first thing he had to do was to keep that promise to his mother. He sat down and read five pages to make up for the days he had skipped. From now on he wouldn't miss a day.

After that he felt better and began to go through everything in the cabin to see exactly what he had on hand, and what use he could make of everything.

And although the bears went away that evening, they were soon to pay Allan a return visit. Only the next time he would not be quite so lucky.

5

First thing the next morning, Allan made a
wooden canvas-covered frame to fit the cabin
window and keep out the frozen wind. Because the ship was so tightly surrounded by
ice, he was afraid that the air inside the cabin
might go bad; so every morning he rolled his
canvas shade partway up. This let a certain
amount of fresh air come in, and also let in
some light. For several days he kept putting
up and taking down the cast-iron grate every
time he left the cabin. But when he no longer
saw any sign of bears in the area, he got tired
of constantly handling the heavy grate and
one day left it down.

The next thing Allan did was to get the door
of the cabin open. It took him a while, for the
door opened outward and was jammed by a
solid wall of ice on the outside. But finally he
got the door off its hinge posts and taken
down. For a moment he stared at the solid ice
that blocked his way.

Ordinarily there was an open deck to cross between the captain's cabin and the forecastle, where the crew slept. But this open area was now packed solid with ice and Allan would have to hack out a tunnel before he could reach the crew's quarters. To make it even worse, the work would have to be done in semidarkness and in bitter cold.

It took him all that day and half of the next day to reach the forecastle. But when he got inside the crew's quarters he was well rewarded. He found some flints to make fire with, his tobacco and pipe, plenty of clothes, pieces of sailcloth, and other useful objects. Most important of all, he found the floor covered with pieces of coal that had spilled out of the coal bin when the ship turned turtle. Underneath everything was an old hatchet that had been used to break up the larger lumps of coal.

He moved all his new possessions to the captain's cabin and spent most of the next day moving all the coal. He could not be sure when the ice overhead might sink down and block up his tunnel. Allan lost no time in lighting a fire. Not wanting to burn a hole in anything, he placed the coals and kindling in the empty biscuit tin. For a while he just sat there, hunched over the fire, enjoying the red glow, the warmth, the tiny flames that licked out between the pieces of coal. He got his hands down close to the heat. Then he took off his boots and stockings and got his feet nice and warm. Next he melted some ice in a billycan, boiled the water, and enjoyed the luxury of his first face and neck wash in over a week.

But with that first fire, Allan ran across a new problem. The cabin filled up with smoke, and to keep from choking he had to crouch on the floor. He badly needed some way to get rid of the smoke. He tried moving his makeshift stove over to the cabin window, but the draft of air coming down the outside tunnel blew the smoke back into his face.

Allan put out the fire and decided he would have to cut a hole in the ceiling. With the ship upside down, the after hold was above him, and he could let the smoke drift up and into the hold.

Of course what was now the ceiling used to be the floor, and Allan had to cut through a layer of heavy carpet and two wooden floor layers before he broke through and into the hold. And here he ran across another problem. Immediately above him were several hundred barrels of whale blubber from the last whale the *Anne Forbes* had captured.

Allan set to work with the tools at hand: the harpoon head, the old hatchet, and his carving knife. Because everything was frozen, including the two-foot squares of whale meat in the barrel, it was like trying to make a hole in cement. In fact sparks sometimes flew when he attacked the frozen wood. After hours of work he managed to break the barrel apart and drag down the frozen chunks of meat. The wood from the barrel he set aside as fuel. He next made a torch from old rags soaked in lamp oil and stuffed into the bottom half of a broken bottle. Lighting his rough torch, he stepped up on a chair and thrust the lamp into the hole. He groaned. The way was blocked by another barrel lying on its side. He had to do the same job all over again, only this time standing on a chair and with hardly any room to use his tools.

He climbed down from the chair and kicked the harpoon head and hatchet out of the way. It was useless; he might as well give up. Every muscle ached and more than anything else he wanted to climb into his closet, pull the covers over his head, and forget that he was still on the *Anne Forbes*. But he sat down on the chair and forced himself to examine his problem. He had often been in that hold, had helped roll in the barrels of whale meat from the last carcass, and he knew that the barrels were stacked three high. Which meant that he had to cut through two more layers before he could break clear and into the empty space in the hold. No, one more, because the last barrel could be pushed aside. Then there would be two or three feet of open space between the barrels and the bottom of the hull. Once he was in that clear space he could crawl over the barrels and break his way into all the other holds of the ship, protected from the elements above by a strong oaken keel.

Wearily he got to his feet, stood up on the chair, and began to try and break apart the next barrel. Hours later he had the second barrel broken up and the frozen blubber pulled down and piled up against the walls of the cabin. As he feared, there was yet another barrel blocking the hole, but this one had nothing on top of it and he was finally able to roll it out of the way. Then he crawled up through the hold and into the clear area above the barrels. In the light of the torch, he could look up at the floor planks laid over the bottom of the ribbed frame. He still had to break through several layers of tough planks to make a hole to the outside.

He climbed back down the hole and dropped into the cabin. He would start to break through the keel tomorrow. At least he now had a way of getting into the other holds of the *Anne Forbes* and did not have to worry that the ice might close in and block his way to the forecastle.

With some wood shavings and lamp oil he managed to get a small coal fire going. While some of the smoke went up through and into the hold above him, most of it gradually filled the cabin until a heavy pall of smoke lay just under the ceiling. Before the smoke got too heavy he had time to hack off a few pieces of whale meat, stick them on the point of his carving knife, and thaw them out over the fire. After nothing but biscuits for the past weeks, the half-raw whale meat tasted delicious and he ate his fill. He stored the rest of the whale meat in the ice tunnel outside the cabin door, read a page of the Bible, and then put out the fire with melted icewater. Then he settled into bed inside the clothes closet, taking with him his flint, a rough torch of oil-soaked rags, and his carving knife, just in case another bear decided to pay him a visit.

The next day Allan went outside, climbed up to the end of the keel, and began to hack a hole in the ship's planking. He swung the hatchet and it bounced off the frozen wood. He swung again and this time managed to cut a few fibers of the tough frozen oak. Furiously he pounded on the keel. The oak was so frozen that he was mashing the wood instead of cutting it. Another blow and the hatchet skidded off the planking and flew out of his hands. Cursing, he scrambled down from the keel to retrieve his axe. By the time he found it, his hands were numb and useless from the cold. He went back inside the cabin, took off his mittens, and warmed his hands over the small coal fire.

All he had to work with was the harpoon head, the coal hatchet, the whaleboat anchor and, his carving knife. He could not work more than ten or fifteen minutes without going inside to thaw out his frozen hands. And there was now only a couple of hours of daylight every day.

The slow and tortuous work took three days but finally he had a fair-sized hole clear through the ship's bottom and into the hold. To his delight he found that his rough chimney now worked beautifully. The smoke was pulled out of the cabin and up into the hold where it soon made its way through the keel and into the sky. For the first time in days the air in the cabin was clear. The new chimney arrangement made Allan happy for another reason. The smoke rising from the keel might now be noticed by a ship that would otherwise pass the iceberg without spotting him.

Remembering all that whale meat in the hold above him, he began to hope that he could make it through the winter on the *Anne Forbes*. In thanksgiving he read several pages of the Bible, drank half a cup of rum to celebrate, then retired to his closet for a good night's sleep. For the first time since the ship went down, Allan felt comfortably warm, well fed, and somewhat hopeful for the future.

The big thing that worried him now was the loneliness. With no one to talk to, to share his problems with, even to argue with, it was hard to keep his spirits up. After a while nothing seemed important anymore if there was no one else around to see how important it was. One thing he had noticed, the time went by a lot faster when he was working hard. During the past three or four days he hadn't once been bothered by the feeling that time was standing still. He would have to line up a whole lot of jobs to do so that he kept himself constantly busy. He would have to make a calendar to keep track of the days. Already he was no longer sure if the *Anne Forbes* struck the iceberg one week or two weeks ago. Tomorrow he would see about making his cabin, especially the closet, as windproof and coldproof as possible. It was the beginning of October, and he had six rough months ahead of him. He would have to be well-prepared to last out the freezing cold and week-long blizzards that were sure to come. And thinking hopefully of the future, Allan fell asleep.

Sometime later he was awakened by sounds outside the closet. He thought he heard heavy breathing, and the sound of something being moved. Or was he just dreaming? He sat up, held his breath, and listened. There was no mistaking that heavy snuffling sound. Another polar bear had entered the cabin!

Allan felt the heavy hand of fear clutch his heart. Maybe if he stayed where he was, and stayed quiet, the bear would go away. Another crash and this time he realized that the bear had found one of his tins of biscuits and was trying to open it. He did not want to leave the closet and try to chase the bear. But neither did he want all his biscuits eaten or ruined. And if he stayed where he was, the animal might decide to break into the closet and then he would be trapped.

As quietly as possible Allan managed to get his torch lit. With the carving knife in one hand and the torch in the other, he kicked open the door and jumped out with a wild yell!

The startled bear stood on his hind legs, looked at Allan, and grunted. Allan stood stock still in his fear. The bear seemed to be ten feet tall, though he later realized that the animal had to be under six feet since that was the distance between the floor and the ceiling of the cabin.

For a long moment bear and Allan looked at each other. A drop of burning oil fell on Allan's hand and he let out a sudden cry. The bear dropped to all fours, whirled around and made for the entrance hole. The animal smashed into the window frame and somehow got tangled up in the canvas flap that covered the hole. The bear's head, one shoulder, and one arm were through the frame but the rest of the body remained in the cabin. For a moment the bear was jammed!

Allan thought of several things at once. The bear might decide to pull back from the hole and turn on him. If he managed to kill the bear he would have fresh meat. He was so frightened that he had to do something. He hurriedly set the torch in the tin box that he used as a stove, ran over and plunged his knife into the bear's side, just beneath the huge white arm. Then, holding on to the bear's back, he sank the knife again and again into the animal's body; into the neck, the side, and the stomach. The bear roared with pain and threw Allan off in its struggles. Allan fell on the stove and the torch went out. For a long moment he lay on the floor of the cabin, out of breath, and wondered what he should do. He almost went back inside his closet, but he realized that, no matter how frightened he was, he could not leave the animal until he was sure that it was fatally wounded. He tried to relight the torch but could not find his flint. Afraid then that the bear might yet work loose and destroy everything in the cabin, including himself, Allan went over to the dim white shape and plunged the knife again and again into the animal's body. Once more Allan was thrown off and once more he returned to the attack, sensing that the animal was growing weaker. In a curious way it was easier to fight the bear in the dark. Allan did not have to look at those curving points of black claws on the ends of the animal's powerful paws. He could not see those fearful teeth, those black lips, and terrible snarl. Finally, after what seemed like hours, the animal stopped its struggles and Allan lay back on the floor, completely done in. It took a good fifteen minutes to recover from his fear. Then he had to pad around in the dark of his closet to find the flint and get the torch relit. As soon as the flame flared brightly in the cabin, he was astonished at the sight that met his eyes. The polar bear had turned completely red! Blood seemed to be on everything. Even his own clothes were soaked with it. And as he watched, a thin trickle of blood ran from the animal's mouth and dripped into a pool on the floor. It was funny, but he hadn't felt the blood when he was attacking the bear. All he had noticed was the animal's fearsome strength and the heavy rank smell that came from its body.

Allan felt wildly happy and desperately sick at the same time. In fact for a moment he thought that he was going to pass out so he drew a half cup of rum and sat down to drink it. After he had gained some control over his nerves, he went over to look at the bear. The animal's black tongue, hanging out of its mouth, had already started to freeze.

Allan was still too excited to go back to bed. So he began to clean and skin the bear. He cut the body into square pieces that he stored, along with the whale blubber, in the ice tunnel just outside the door. There the meat would freeze and be available any time he wanted it. It took him several hours to finish the job. He skinned out the fur and spread it on hooks on the wall of the cabin. When it was dry, and all of the blood washed out of it, it would make a good robe for his bed. He figured that he had at least two hundred pounds of fresh meat now stored away and he knew that fresh meat was important. Although he guessed there was plenty of salted meat somewhere on the *Anne Forbes,* a diet of salt meat and ship biscuits, without any fruit or vegetables, usually led to scurvy, and scurvy was a disease that often proved fatal.

When everything was cleaned up and put away, Allan went to his entrance hole, climbed through the snow tunnel, and went outside. Daybreak had come and it was going to be a beautiful sunny day, even though it would still be cold. He climbed up on top of the keel and looked around. The *Anne Forbes* was now so well locked into the ice that Allan could not spot the open sea anywhere. They were frozen fast for at least the next six months.

The cold soon drove Allan back inside. This time he put up the iron grate, as well as the canvas covering. And while the grate might not keep out a really determined bear, it might slow him up enough to let Allan find some other way to stop the animal from entering. Allan realized that his open snow tunnel looked like a possible cave opening to bears, which might be why they were attracted to the cabin window. Or it might be the smell of whale blubber being carried on the smoke that rose up through the hold and out the opening in the keel. And that smell would probably carry for miles, which meant that he could expect more visits from wandering and hungry bears.

Allan opened the closet door and settled under the covers, trying to make up for lost sleep. But his body had still not unwound from the fight with the bear, so he lay awake there in the darkness for another hour before finally drifting off.

And in his sleep he dreamed that someone was calling his name from a great distance, someone who kept crying and crying and would not stop.

6

Allan woke up to the sound of that someone crying. For a long moment he lay inside the closet and listened to the cries. Was it a wolf? Or did wolves ever come this far into the polar regions? More likely an Arctic fox, or perhaps a bird of some kind. He didn't think the sound came from inside the cabin, but just in case his fingers closed around the handle of the carving knife. Was another bear trying to break in?

He opened the closet door and looked over at the window. It was undisturbed, and now it was clear that the sounds — whimpers and sniffles and groans — were coming from the outside snow entrance to the window. The cries sounded almost human.

Several times he shouted. For a moment or so there would be silence, then the funny whimpering noises would start all over again. Finally Allan's curiosity got the better of him. Carving knife in hand, he cautiously opened the canvas frame of the window. At first he saw nothing, then a whimper caused him to look down. There, sitting on the floor of the snow tunnel, was a polar bear cub. Its fore-paws were up and covering its head, making it look like a little white ball of fur.

For a minute Allan felt terrible. He realized immediately that the animal he killed the night before must have been the cub's mother. Tenderly he picked up the tiny animal and brought it inside the cabin. He set the cub on the floor and the animal began to sniff at everything in sight, as though searching for someone. It was heartrending and Allan felt worse yet. Then the animal reached the hanging bearskin and bleated with joy. It clung to the skin, tried to lick the fur, and whimpered over and over again.

Allan lifted the cub from its mother's fur The animal weighed about thirty pounds and Allan guessed that it was only two or three months old. He offered some biscuits and the cub gobbled them down. Then Allan thought of the whale blubber in the ice tunnel. He hacked some pieces out of a frozen chunk, lit a fire, and thawed out the whale meat.

The small animal looked like a very fat medium-sized white dog. It was a female, so Allan decided to call her *Nancy*, after his girl-friend back in Aberdeen. He kept petting the animal, stroking its fur, and calling it "Nancy." In between pettings he fed the cub small pieces of whale meat, which Nancy gratefully chewed and swallowed. Allan was careful not to let her eat as much as she wanted, afraid that too much might make her sick.

Every once in a while Nancy would run over to the hanging fur and lick it, then begin to whimper again. Allan took the skin down off the hooks and spread it on the floor. Nancy sniffed it all over. Finally she curled up on the middle of the fur and went to sleep.

Allan sat down in his chair and tried to figure out what to do with his pet. Until last night he had almost stopped worrying about polar bears. He had heard that they hibernated during the winter, sleeping right through the cold months until spring came. Nancy must have been born somewhat late in the season, which was why the mother bear had been late in finding a den for the winter. She had probably wanted to get Nancy as big and strong as possible before they holed up for the cold months. But would Nancy now act as a bear and go to sleep for the winter? Or would she, without her mother to guide and protect her, follow the same sleeping habits that Allan did?

If Nancy could live on biscuits and whale blubber, then Allan had no doubt that she would stay with him. But what would happen when Nancy grew into a full-size bear? By then, with any luck, he would be off his iceberg prison. In the meantime he was grateful for her company, even if she did decide to sleep through the whole winter. He no longer felt the piercing misery of being completely alone.

The next morning Nancy was still sleeping and Allan decided not to bother her. He would let her wake up naturally. Crouched down in front of her, he stroked the thick fur and felt a kinship for the poor orphan, cut off from her own kind. Wasn't he an orphan himself, just as much cut off from his people? Nancy was all he had now as far as kinfolk was concerned, and he was all the poor brute had for a relative.

"Aye, lass, we're in a pretty pickle, the pair of us," he said to Nancy. "From now on I'll have to be half bear and you half human if we're to get along in each other's company."

In the meantime, while Nancy slept, he would get busy and fix up the cabin. The carpeting on the ceiling — he would pull that all down and use it on the floor. Beneath the floor there were tons of ice and the carpeting would help protect his feet against the cold. It would also make it a little more comfortable for Nancy.

He started to pull down the carpeting and was surprised to find, under one corner, a small trap door. The captain had other ways of getting into the holds and obviously did not need to use the trap door and therefore did not mind it being covered with carpeting. But for a moment it made Allan angry with himself. After all that hard work to chop a hole through the ceiling, there had been a trapdoor. If he had not been so lazy that first week, he would have discovered it sooner and saved himself a lot of work.

He managed to get the trapdoor open, and it hung down by two hinges. Above were more barrels of whale meat, but after some hard work he got them shifted out of the way. He was now in the clear space below the keel and able to explore the length of the vessel. He made his way from one hold to the next and finally reached the hold where most of the ship's supplies had been stored. To his great joy he discovered all kinds of useful things. There were barrels of freshwater, now turned to ice. He found plenty of coal. There were several casks of salted beef and a half barrel of salt pork, as well as several barrels of flour and a barrel of oatmeal. There was bacon, mutton, and deer meat, as well as more ship's biscuits. He found half a barrel of Scotch whiskey, along with several boxes of tobacco, a box of snuff, and a small wooden box full of clay pipes. The pipes were packed in wood shavings and were called *halfpenny pipes* by the sailors since they only cost a halfpenny each. Most sailors used these pipes because they were so cheap that a sailor did not mind if he lost or broke one. The wood shavings Allan kept. When dried out they would be very useful for starting his fire.

He was able to go from the provision hold into the crew's quarters and here he also found many things overlooked on his last visit, including an axe and a chest of tools that had belonged to the ship's carpenter. He also found several lamps and plenty of whale oil to fill them with.

He found two stoves, one in the ship's galley and one in the forecastle, but both were too large and too heavy to move by himself. He did manage to salvage several lengths of stovepipe, which he later ran up through the hold above the cabin and out through the keel. This made his chimney work even better, and now that he had a frying pan and several copper pots from the cook's galley, he was able to cook rough-and-ready meals on his homemade tin-box stove.

One of the many useful things that Allan found was a sailor's "hussuf," a canvas wallet that contained several needles, spools of thread, an assortment of buttons, darning wool and a small pair of scissors. *"Hussuf"* was a nickname for *"housewife,"* and a sailor, who never had his wife along on a voyage, would jokingly call his packet of materials for making repairs on his clothing his "housewife."

Allan knew he would find the hussuf very useful for making backpacks out of sailcloth. When spring came he'd need them to carry his food supplies when he tried to hike out and find land.

At first Allan thought it odd that he found no bodies of his former shipmates. Then he realized that his warning cry of "Berg ahead!" must have gotten them up on deck. When the *Anne Forbes* hit the wall of ice, anyone left below deck would surely have come up to find out what the vessel had crashed into. They must all have drowned in the sea, though he sometimes wondered, remembering the corpses the bears had found, if the body of Alex the cook, or Chips the carpenter, or even Big Tom the first mate, might not be frozen into the ice somewhere near or even right under the *Anne Forbes.*

Several days passed and Nancy slept on. Sometimes she was so still that Allan could not make out her breathing, nor feel the play of her lungs, and he would fear that she had died in her sleep. But then he would place his open hand right in front of her nostrils and always, within a minute or so, he would feel the faint warming of her breath on his palm.

On the fourth day after he had found Nancy, and when she still showed no signs of waking up, Allan decided to rouse her from her sleep. He was afraid that she might not yet be strong enough to survive hibernation without more food. He also wanted to see what she was like, to talk to her and watch her funny way of walking, to see the comical way she sometimes sat down. He was lonely for her company.

He leaned forward and called, "Nancy! Nancy! Wake up, c'mon, that's a good wee lassie."

Allan soon found that waking Nancy was no simple matter. No matter how he called her, how he shook her, she refused to fully open her eyes. All he could get out of her were a couple of moans. Finally he hit on a simple idea. He lit his pipe and blew tobacco smoke into her nose. Nancy gave a hearty sneeze and Allan blew more smoke into her nostrils. Another half dozen sneezes and she began to wake up. At the first sign that she was coming to, Allan opened her mouth and popped a piece of whale meat between her jaws.

"There Nancy, chew on that for a while."

She began to chew on the meat and Allan

fed her four or five more pieces until she was fully awake.

"Feeling better?" he asked.

Nancy's answer was another tremendous sneeze.

Allan laughed. "That's more like it. Here, have another piece." He fed her a couple of pounds of whale meat but again did not give her too much.

When Nancy had finished eating, Allan expected her to go back to sleep but she fooled him. Instead she wandered around the cabin several times, sniffing at everything her little black button of a nose came in touch with. She came back to where Allan was sitting, flopped down, and began to chew on his boot. He leaned down and scratched her on the head and her eyes closed for a moment with contentment.

"Aye, lass," Allan murmured, "there's a lot to be said for being a poor dumb brute. You'll not be bothered with memories of a better life."

For the next week or so Nancy stayed awake when Allan was awake, and slept when Allan slept. Then she went into another deep sleep that lasted three or four days before Allan again woke her up to give her more whale meat. For the rest of the winter she had three or four periods of deep sleep that lasted as long as a week. But in between her hibernating periods, she only slept when Allan did, and followed him everywhere he went. She loved to wrestle with him on the floor of the cabin and Allan often thought that if anything kept him alive, it was having Nancy to look after and to talk to.

And so Allan kept busy. He had to cook his meals and clean the cabin. Weather permitting, there was his daily walk to the iceberg mountain for a look around the area. He continued to explore as much of the ship as he could and constantly found things that were useful. On one trip to the forecastle he found a sort of early shotgun, called a *fowling piece*, and some lead balls. On another trip he found a box of gunpowder. The gunpowder had been soaked in seawater, but by degrees he managed to get all of it dried out. He also found many of the tools used in whaling: harpoons, lances, cutting knives, blubber hooks, even a pedal-operated grindstone. The grinding wheel was broken, the stone having cracked in two when the *Anne Forbes* turned upside down. Allan didn't mind that, of course, he could still sharpen his knives by hand on one of the broken halves of the stone.

He scratched out a calendar on the wall of the cabin but after a couple of weeks he gave up trying to keep track of the days. The Arctic night had already set in, and he had no way of telling night from day. Neither did he have a clock or watch. He was often unsure as to how much time had passed. He might sleep two hours and think he had slept eight, or sleep ten hours and think he had slept only two. The occasional heavy snowstorms did not bother him; in fact he looked forward to them as he noticed that the snow piled on the up-turned bottom of his ship helped to keep the cabin warm. Sometimes, after a storm, when the fire did not draw properly, he would have to go outside and clear the blocked end of the chimney pipe of snow. Generally though, the fierce winds blew all of the snow away from the keel of the *Anne Forbes*. The ship was too exposed, miles from any land mass that would help break the force of the winter winds.

In fact Allan was almost comfortable in his cabin. He found that a mixture of coal and whale blubber made a nice burning fire. And even on those bitterly cold days, when the temperature fell to forty or fifty below zero and the fire couldn't keep the cabin warm, he could always go to bed. There, buried under layer after layer of carpeting and clothing, his body heat would be enough to keep him fairly comfortable. And when all else failed, he could always fall back on a cup of rum to ward off the cold.

Nancy, of course, was not bothered by the extreme temperatures. She now had her own sleeping corner, piled high with old bedclothes, right beside Allan's closet.

Allan knew that somehow he would have to get through the long winter. Then surely when spring came, and the whaling fleets returned to the Greenland fishery, a passing ship would pick up his signal, lower a boat, and pluck him off his icy prison.

7

It was now the time of the long arctic night, from mid-November to the end of January, when the sun was completely absent from the sky. On clear days, however, Allan could still tell where the sun was hiding as the sky above the horizon at that point was a lighter shade of blue than the rest of the heavens.

On clear days and nights he often left the *Anne Forbes* to watch the exciting display of aurora borealis, those waving bands and shimmering curtains of colored light that arched across the sky in ever changing patterns. There were still and windless nights when the frozen sea seemed to glow from inside, now a pink color and now a light blue as the ice reflected the moonlight or starshine or the dancing show of northern lights. At such times Allan was almost thankful he was on the *Anne Forbes*. Otherwise he would never have known the beauty of those northern nights, a beauty that sometimes took his breath away and made him want to weep.

But there were other times, especially when Nancy was in one of her deep sleeps and the wind howled for days without letup, that he really did weep — from despair. And although he had plenty of food a sort of weakness came over him and he did not want to leave his closet. He did not want to go outside. He had no appetite and no desire to do anything except stay beneath the bedclothes. He wished that he could sleep for a week at a time, like Nancy, and sometimes he even imagined, after twenty-four hours inside the closet, that he had learned how to hibernate. But that was silly, of course, because he knew that he was awake most of the time.

Sometimes it was Nancy waking up that pulled him out of one of his bad moods. Or sometimes it was a clear windless day or night that drew him outside to marvel at the beauty of the ice, or the vast millions of stars in the mysterious black vault of the velvet skies. Sometimes, for no reason at all, he would come out of his black mood and start to dream up all kinds of plans to make life more comfortable and more interesting on the *Anne Forbes.*

Allan spent a lot of his time in training Nancy. He taught her such words as *stay, sit, stand,* and so on. She began to gain weight very quickly and soon she was the size of a small calf. She often followed Allan out of the wreck and around on the ice. Sometimes she tried to dig down through the ice as though she were trying to get into the sea, but the ice was far too thick for her. She loved to roll around on the drifts of snow behind ice floes and could not understand why Allan would not wrestle with her in the snow. At the bottom of the ice mountain there was a clear slope of ice about fifty feet long, and Nancy loved to climb to the top of the slope, sit down and slide to the bottom on her back, her four paws up in the air. She looked so comical on her slide that Allan never tired of watching her.

He found Nancy very gentle and never once did she show any signs of turning on him, of trying to claw or bite him. Like a dog she would sometimes take Allan's hand in her mouth, but so gently that her sharp teeth never broke the skin. She often tried to imitate Allan and learned to walk erect for short distances. On some moonlit days Allan would take Nancy outside and tell her to stand. Then he would link arms with her and give the command, "Walk." He and Nancy would then go for a short stroll over the ice, looking, for all the world, like a stuffy old married couple taking a Sunday walk in his native Aberdeen.

Nancy looked so funny, waddling along arm in arm with Allan that he often broke into fits of laughing. And Nancy would even try to imitate his laugh. She would squeeze up her face and nose, half close her eyes, and give a whinny that sounded exactly like a horse.

At such times, watching Nancy try so hard to imitate her master, Allan felt a pure love for his pet. One thing he was positive of, no matter how short he ran on food, he would never kill Nancy to save himself. It would be like killing a brother, or a sister.

And so the winter wore away and the light patch in the southern sky grew brighter and brighter. Allan now found it very hard to make up his mind what to do. He wanted to strike out for land, while the sea ice was still frozen. But he had no idea in which direction to find the shore, and he did not know how far he might have to travel. And even should he find land, how would he live when he got there? Allan knew of Eskimos, of course. They sometimes traded animal skins and furs to the captains of whaling ships. But on her last trip the *Anne Forbes* had been at sea the whole time so that Allan had never actually seen an Eskimo. And Eskimos were few and far between in the polar regions. He could wander around until long after his food was all gone before he met any of those strange inhabitants of the Arctic. And even should he fall in with a band of Eskimos, it might be years before the Eskimos came into contact with any Europeans.

But if he stayed on the iceberg and kept a sharp lookout, he should be able to spot a sailing vessel either on its way to or back from the whaling grounds. There were at least two dozen whaling ships that made the round trip every year from Scotland and England, and twice as many Dutch whalers, not to mention the occasional French, German, or American ship that came up to try its luck. If he climbed to the peak of his ice mountain and planted a signal flag there, surely it would be noticed by one of the whaling ships. And if he himself spotted a ship far out to sea, he could light a fire and burn two or three pounds of oakum, which threw off a dense black smoke that would be visible for miles. He had found over a hundred pounds of oakum in one of the holds, so he had plenty of material to make smoke signals with. But staying on the iceberg had its dangers too. The *Anne Forbes*, loosened from the grip of the winter ice, would probably sink. And how could he survive with the *Anne Forbes* gone? Then too, the iceberg might get caught in a south-flowing current, drift down to warmer waters, and melt.

It was a hard decision to make, either to

leave the comfort and security of the *Anne Forbes* and strike out on his own over the unknown ice or to take his chances on the iceberg.

One day, on his trip over to the ice mountain to replenish his water supplies, he got an idea that helped to make up his mind. When it looked as though the sea ice were breaking up, he would shift his living quarters to the peak of the iceberg.

For the next three days the weather was stormy, the wind blowing so hard that the loose snow made it impossible to see more than a step or two ahead on the ice. For three days Allan stuck to the cabin on the *Anne Forbes*. Anxious to get going on his plan, he started out for the ice mountain as soon as the weather cleared. He and Nancy left the ship, and Allan noticed, as he hiked over the ice, that the light patch in the southern sky had turned to orange. The color gradually built to a fiery red that lit up the whole sky and faded away in the north to a dying pale pink. He had just about reached the iceberg mountain when the sun put in an appearance, a glowing scarlet tip of a fingernail that rested on the horizon.

"Ah, Nancy lass, there it is again, the lovely sun!" He threw his arms around Nancy and hugged her.

Nancy took the hug as an invitation to wrestle and promptly dumped her master on his backside. For a moment they rolled over and over on the ice, Allan letting out whoops of joy. He got to his feet and managed to calm down his pet. Then he spent the next hour or so just watching the sun. The sunrise soon turned into a sunset as the topmost rim of the sun dipped again beneath the horizon. In the space of less than an hour Allan had seen both a sunrise and a sunset! And while he hated to see the sun go away, he knew that on each succeeding day the glowing orange ball would climb higher and higher into the sky, filling the whole northern world with its promise of light and warmth.

"Now then, lass, you've seen your first sunrise," Allan said to his pet.

Nancy whinnied.

Allan looked up at the ice mountain. His whole body seemed to be flooded with new energy.

"We'll carve out steps to the top of yon peak," he said, his staff pointing upward. "We'll make a house up there, so we will, a wee cave house for the summer and, Nancy love, we'll sit up there in cool and splendid ease, and we'll eat the best of food, and drink an odd snort of rum to keep out the damp. And we'll have a lovely high seat to watch for the whaling fleet. Oh aye, but we'll have a glorious time, the two of us."

Nancy took his hand in her mouth and tugged.

"You're anxious to start, is that it?"

It took Allan a couple of weeks of hard work to chip out steps to the top of the ice mountain. His flight of steps wound in and out of deep cracks in the face of the berg. Twenty or so feet beneath the peak, where the ice was still thick, he began to hollow out a cave. He now had plenty of tools from the *Anne Forbes* to work with, and on days when the weather was not too cold, and there was enough light, he hacked away at his cave hollow.

A couple of months later his ice cave actually had two rooms, a tiny back sleeping room and a larger front room that served as a kitchen and lookout point. As the days grew longer, Allan kept bringing more and more supplies to the ice mountain. He brought carpeting and extra bedclothes, coal and whale blubber for a fire, one of his lamps and a supply of oil, a box of ship biscuits, and several bottles full of rum. He brought some frozen meat and a long lance pole from one of the holds. Almost on the very tip of the iceberg, he drilled a small hole in the ice and put up his lance pole. On top of the pole he tied one of the captain's red shirts as a signal to any ships that might be passing by. But he found that the wind soon tore the shirt to shreds, so he left the pole bare, meaning to attach a flag of sorts once the sea was clear of ice and therefore safe for navigation.

And now with the coming of spring and the increasing chance of rescue, Allan's thoughts turned more and more to that other Nancy, his Nancy of the red-gold hair and large blue eyes.

He first met her the day he walked past the front door of Maclean's Drapery Shop and saw her standing just inside the entrance. She was sweeping the floor, and he noticed the splotches of damp here and there on the floorboards, where used tea leaves from the morning's breakfast had been scattered to keep down the dust.

At the time he had just turned fourteen and was finishing his second year in Craigie's Tailoring Establishment. He had heard that Maclean's was getting a new shopgirl but he had thought that the new girl would be much older. At that first sight of Nancy, he fell head over heels in love. From one of the other shop assistants he found out her name, Nancy Campion. From then on, every excuse he got, he went parading past the drapery-shop windows. One day he talked Mister Craigie into allowing him to take his horse to the blacksmith for new shoes. On that glorious day, seated casually on the bare back of the powerful horse, he managed to parade past Maclean's and be twice seen by Nancy, once on his way going and once coming back. And on the return voyage, noting her standing just inside the doorway of the shop, he had swept off his cloth cap and called down from the back of the horse, "Brave day, Miss Campion."

She had smiled, blushed, then run back into the shop.

Unfortunately, because he worked indoors at Craigie's, he did not have too many chances of seeing her. Of course he always volunteered to run up to Maclean's when Mister Craigie ran out of buttons, or thread, or linen stiffening, or chalk, but Mister Craigie always liked to do his own buying in the drapery store.

However there was one time of the day he could count on seeing her, at eight o'clock in the morning when he swept the wooden sidewalk in front of Craigie's. A hundred yards up the street Nancy would be doing the same job outside her shop. And after they had both swept their stretches of sidewalk, Nancy sweeping down and he sweeping up, they would, more often than not, lean on their brooms for a little while and look at each other. And those were the most precious moments of the day for Allan. If he heard a cart coming down the street he would hold his breath until it passed Maclean's. Then he had to pray that the man did not want to stop at the tailor's. And how he groaned when the cart stopped in front of Craigie's, for he knew he would have to go inside and see what the man wanted. But if the cart rattled on past, then how precious those extra few moments were, leaning on his broom and looking up at his Nancy. And how, for the rest of the day, he would treasure that little wave she gave him when she finally had to go back inside the shop.

"Ah, Nancy, Nancy, but those were innocent days for both of us," he cried out.

And Nancy his pet came waddling over to where he stood at the foot of the ice mountain. She thrust her moist black nose into his hand.

Allan looked out over the frozen wastes of ice. He was a long way from the bustling streets of Aberdeen. A sudden gust of wind brought tears to his eyes. He turned away, hunched his shoulders, and struggled back to the empty hulk of the *Anne Forbes*.

8

There were seven of them and they were flying so low that he might have reached up and pulled one of them down. He was standing just outside the snow entrance to the cabin when he heard a soft, irregular clapping. Then they were upon him, seven gleaming white snow geese with black wing tips, seven hurtling bodies swerving away at the last moment to gain altitude as they pumped northward in a tight V, one bird in the lead and three stepping back on each flank.

He sent a long ringing cheer after them. "Ah, the lovely brave geese!" he cried out. "Welcome, welcome back!"

The sight of the birds filled his heart with hope. With the exception of a solitary gull, they were the only sign of life he had seen in months. To celebrate their arrival, he went back inside the cabin, drew a half cup of rum for himself, and cut a large piece of whale meat for Nancy. Then he and Nancy went outside and sat on top of the exposed keel of the ship. Allan sipped the rum. He felt like dancing. It was so good to see other forms of life again!

And in the days that followed, wild ducks and Canada geese flew over on their way to the northern nesting grounds. Night after night the fulmars and Arctic terns and kittiwakes made the skies hum with the beat of their wings.

Soon the ice beneath the *Anne Forbes* was constantly growling and crackling. One day, afraid that the ice might suddenly loosen and the *Anne Forbes* go down, Allan shifted his living quarters to the top of the iceberg. Not many days later he saw a ribbon of clear water to the south and realized that the winter ice was breaking up. It was too late now to try and reach land. For the next six months his only hope of getting off the iceberg would be if he were spotted by a whaling ship.

One night soon after, as Allan was sleeping in his cave room on the iceberg peak, he felt the whole ice mountain give a violent tilt. The sudden movement jolted him awake and he sat up and lit the lamp. Nancy had also awakened, and he looked over at her and asked, "Well, lass, if the whole berg turns bottom up, what are we going to do?"

Nancy had no interest in the matter. Sitting

down, she lazily scratched the underside of her chin with a front paw.

"Or has the *Anne Forbes* broken loose and finally gone to the bottom?"

But whatever had happened, for the moment there was nothing Allan could do. He would not take a chance on going down his ice stairway in the dark. For the next hour or so there were several smaller shakes and lifting movements, but finally all was still again.

As soon as there was enough light in the morning, Allan went to the door of his cave and looked out. The iceberg had broken loose from the surrounding ice pan and already a channel of clear water showed on one side of the berg. Further out, the whole ice field was breaking up with thousands of floes bobbing up and down in the water.

Worried about the *Anne Forbes*, Allan hurried down to the bottom of the ice mountain and made his way over to the ship. Although the *Anne Forbes* was still locked in the grip of the ice, open water could be seen just a few feet beyond the upturned keel. It was at this moment Allan realized that the ship had to be resting on an underwater ledge of the iceberg. Perhaps, he thought, the *Anne Forbes* was not doomed after all, perhaps she might stay put throughout the whole summer.

In the meantime Nancy had spotted the

open water on the other side of the *Anne Forbes*. She galumped off in that direction and Allan followed her. When Nancy reached the edge of the water she slid in head first and disappeared. Allan waited at the lip of the iceberg. Nancy was under for so long that he began to worry. Just about when he decided that something had happened to his pet, Nancy's sleek head broke the surface of the water. She had a fish in her mouth. She swam over and laid it on the ice in front of Allan. The fish, a large Arctic char, flopped a couple of times, and Allan put his foot down on top of it. Then he reached over and patted Nancy on the head. "Oh you're a good wee lass. That's it, now fetch another."

A swirl of water and Nancy was gone again. In the next half hour she caught a dozen fish. Allan fed half of them to Nancy and took the rest home and cleaned and gutted them. He had a fresh fish for dinner that night, and it tasted delicious. Strangely enough, on a vessel that worked in some of the richest fishing grounds in the world, Allan had not been able to find even one fishing hook.

He had no trouble freezing and storing the fish. He hollowed out a small square area in one of the ice walls of his cave and stuck the fish in there. For the rest of the summer, as long as there was open water nearby, Nancy caught more than enough for both of them.

The extra fish he cleaned and froze for later.

She also tried to catch seals that came up to sunbathe on the iceberg. But these sleek animals were too quick and wary for her and could easily outswim Nancy in the water. Walrus sometimes came to the berg, but Nancy was too small yet to tackle a full grown walrus.

There was still plenty of loose ice in the open sea, and indeed Allan was never to see the water completely free of ice floes or icebergs, even in the middle of summer. And although his ice island now floated completely on its own, free of any ice fields, it was still at the mercy of ocean tides and winds and currents. And so the iceberg moved now one way and now another.

Allan's biggest worry was that the ledge of ice on which the *Anne Forbes* rested would break off the main body of the iceberg. If that happened he would lose the ship. It was mainly for this reason that he moved so much food and supplies to his cave on top of the ice mountain. However, as the summer wore on he grew more confident that the underwater ledge would hold, that the *Anne Forbes* would stay where she was. Indeed, on one or two occasions during bad storms, Allan slept on the ship rather than in his ice cave.

Another of Allan's worries was that the iceberg would drift to the south, reach warmer water, and rapidly melt. However he soon realized that the iceberg did not drift in any one direction for very long. And while it often drifted south for a day or two, the berg was just as likely to drift west or even north.

Early one morning, when the summer was well advanced, Allan woke up and, following his usual custom, went immediately outside to the ice platform to search the surrounding sea for the sign of a sail. The first thing he noticed was a long, low ridge on the western horizon. Was it land? Or another iceberg? For a moment he cursed the captain for having brought his spyglass up on deck just before the *Anne Forbes* hit. And anyway, what kind of captain sailed with only one telescope?

All day Allan anxiously watched the black line to the west. By nightfall it had definitely grown larger and had taken on the appearance of a body of land. Allan even fancied he could see a shingled beach!

He was so excited that he hardly slept at all that night. Long before sunrise he was out on the observation platform, waiting. As the night blue paled into gray, the outline of land gradually became firm. When it was fully light, he saw that the iceberg had drifted to within less than a mile of a large body of land.

Looking at the high, dark, stone cliffs across from the berg, watching water break on a low shingled beach at the foot of the cliff, Allan began to curse his stupidity in not having made a small boat or raft of some kind. By noon he was positive that the berg's drift was no longer toward land. He knew, or guessed, that the iceberg was a hundred feet deep below the waterline and was probably now hung up on the shallow bottom that shelved out from the land. But without a boat of some kind, that mile might as well be a hundred.

In midafternoon he spotted movement on the beach. A dark bulky figure that he took to be an Eskimo woman was gathering something from the rocks.

As soon as she looked over, Allan stood up on the platform outside his cave and cupped his hands around his mouth. Then he cut loose with the loudest roar that he could manage. "Halooo! Halooo!"

The woman looked up and over at the iceberg. At that moment Nancy came out of the cave and, imitating her beloved master, stood up on her hind legs and also let out a loud roar.

The woman promptly turned around and ran away as fast as she could.

"Come back!" Allan shouted.

In less than a minute the running figure was lost to sight. Allan sank down and buried his head in his hands. Nancy had obviously terrified the woman out of her wits. He might hope that she had gone for help, but it was obvious that she had been badly frightened.

Allan did not know it, of course, but it was probable that the woman mistook him for a polar bear as he often wore his bear rug around his shoulders as a cape. She had probably set off for her village to tell the male hunters that she had seen two polar bears. Polar bears were a great source of meat for Eskimos and they hunted them at every opportunity.

Allan kept a close watch on the beach for the rest of the afternoon but no one else showed up. Toward nightfall the wind shifted, and the berg began to drift out to sea again.

The next morning the empty seas stretched away on every side of the ice island. Allan took a long look around, then went down to the *Anne Forbes* and retired to his sleeping closet. He did not want to go outside, even to take a look around. Why bother? There was nothing out there anyway.

He stayed several days in his closet and might have stayed even longer had it not been for Nancy. During the third day she began to whimper for him, and he finally had to get up and reassure her that nothing was wrong.

Even though something was, for he was very afraid now that he would never get off the iceberg alive.

9

It took Allan several weeks to regain his former good spirits. Before the summer was over he was to see land once again, though this time the berg never got any closer than ten or fifteen miles.

In the meantime Allan began to think of building a boat, or at least a raft. He emptied eight barrels of their whale-meat cargo, sealed the barrels again, and used oakum and hot tar to make them watertight. Then he ripped planking out of the forecastle until he had enough to nail into a rough platform. With a coil of rope he lashed all eight barrels together, then tied the platform to the barrels, making himself a raft. Next he fashioned a long steering tiller out of a couple of planks, made a small mast from a harpoon lance, and sewed together a canvas sail to fit his square-rigged vessel.

He kept the raft, its single sail furled, on

top of the ice, firmly tied to the keel of the *Anne Forbes*. Several times he was tempted to load the raft with supplies and strike out. But then he realized that he might be weeks on the seas before he made land, and he did not want to be cast up on some desolate shore, starving to death, and with no strength left to help himself. Anyway he feared the raft would be of little use in high seas, or over long distances, though it would surely get him a few hundred yards to shore, or keep him alive for another couple of days if anything happened to the *Anne Forbes* and his ice island.

During the summer Allan had plenty of company. There was Nancy, who followed him wherever he went. She did not show any signs of missing her own kind, or wanting to leave the iceberg, though Allan suspected that her feelings would change once she grew to full size. But in the meantime she was good company and Allan often held long conversations with her.

Then too there was plenty of wildlife. He often saw seals sleeping on pans of ice. Small herds of walrus sometimes used the iceberg as a resting platform, between dives to the sea floor after clams and other shellfish. Birds of all descriptions flew over and often landed briefly on his ice island. On several occasions Allan spotted the high feather of mist that came from a sounding whale, and once he even saw the long twisting single horn of a narwahl.

And so Allan and Nancy continued to drift through the polar seas for the rest of the summer. Actually the iceberg was free of sea ice for only a month or so in late July and early August. Indeed, during an exceptionally cold summer, the sea ice sometimes did not break up at all. As the days grew shorter and the ice began to build out again from the edges of the berg, Allan kept a particularly sharp watch for passing sails. The whaling ships would soon be setting their sights on home. He now spent most of his time up in the ice cave, constantly searching the seas for that telltale patch of white that meant a sail.

One day, while Allan was foraging for something on the *Anne Forbes,* he heard a sudden roaring grinding noise that seemed to come from the iceberg tip. He was well used to the various sounds that the ice constantly made: the tinkling sounds of skim ice breaking up, like a thousand drinking glasses shattering all at once; the occasional heavy and solid bump as a large ice floe hit the edge of the iceberg; the single sharp *crack* and heavy swoosh that accompanied a lifting motion under his feet as a section of the iceberg broke off to become what sailors called a *growler.* But this sound was different, like a constant roll of thunder far away. He hurried over to the ice mountain and climbed up to his cave. There below him, on the southern side of the berg, he found the answer. Hundreds of ice floes of all shapes and sizes were being driven up on the iceberg lip. They tumbled over one another, making hills and valleys as they gradually extended the size of the iceberg. The berg was starting to freeze in again for the winter even though it was only mid-September as far as Allan could tell from the length of the days.

And with that Allan realized that the all-too-short Arctic summer was over. The whaling ships would now be setting sail for home, those that had not already left. His chances of being rescued by a ship were practically gone. He would have to spend another terrible winter in his ice prison. He had been a castaway now for a full year and the thought of starting another year on the iceberg made him desperately unhappy.

Yet two days later, having practically given up all hope of ever seeing another ship, he happened to look out over the water and spot a tiny triangle of white dancing on the horizon line to the east. Working as fast as he could, he got a fire going in the mouth of the cave and threw a couple of pounds of greasy oakum on to the coals. Soon thick black smoke was rising high above the iceberg. He climbed up above the cave, lowered the flagpole, and tied the captain's red shirt to the end of the lance, then hoisted the signal again.

For several moments he watched the faraway white butterfly that seemed to have landed on the horizon line and folded shut its wings. Then he hurried down to the *Anne Forbes,* lit a fire in the cabin, and piled more oakum on top. Soon another black column of smoke was climbing into the heavens.

Once more he hurried back to his cave on the ice mountain. Why wasn't that ship heading about? She had to be a whaler, and because her course was probably set for home and the day was fair, she probably only had one masthead aloft. If she were still seeking whales there would be three lookouts above on the masts.

Allan sent prayer after prayer across the water to the masthead on the whaler. Ah now, lad, look this way, he silently begged the sailor. Look man, can't you see the signal? Do you not see the smoke? Yes, that's it, right over here. Now lean out over your rail and sing out, "Smoke on the starboard bow! Distress flag! Castaway!"

But no matter how Allan prayed, that tiny triangle got smaller and smaller until the sinking sun was so low that its rays blinded the whaler lookout from seeing anything to the west.

"May you hit a berg and go straight to the

bottom, you blind pig!" Allan screamed his bitterness after the departing ship. For a wild moment he was about to launch his raft until common sense convinced him that he could not possibly overtake the ship.

He called Nancy and together they went back to the *Anne Forbes*. Allan added a few coals to the fire and put on some fish that Nancy had caught earlier in the day. After supper he had a smoke of his pipe and took out his Bible. He tried to read but he could not get his mind off the whaler, with the wind crowding her sails, hurrying her home.

"Aye, lass, we'll not see another ship for a good wee while I'm thinking," he said aloud to his companion.

When he turned around to look at Nancy she was sitting on the floor, her back to the wall, her head sunk on her chest in her usual taking-a-nap position. She looked so comical that Allan had to laugh.

Nancy heard his laugh and opened her eyes. Then she screwed up her face and gave her special whinny. Allan laughed again, and again Nancy imitated him. For the next five minutes the cabin rang with Allan's laughter and Nancy's imitations.

After that Allan felt much better. He jumped to his feet and shook his fist at all the Arctic seas and lands. "You've haven't got Allan Gordon yet!" he cried out to his enemies. "Aye, not by a long shot. Do you hear me back there in Aberdeen? Do you hear me, master? Allan Gordon will be back!"

Nancy shuffled over, hooked her front paw around Allan's leg, and suddenly tumbled him to the floor. Then she sat on his chest.

"Aye," Allan said. "I'm a right fearsome terror when even a baby bear can best me."

To which Nancy replied with a thorough licking of Allan's face while he tried to scramble out from under and get to his feet.

10

And so Allan resigned himself to staying put for another winter. While he never went any further from his upside-down vessel than the nearby ice mountain, and the *Anne Forbes* stayed locked in the solid ice, this did not mean that Allan's home remained in the same spot all the time.

The ice was always moving, and indeed on the coldest day of winter, when the temperature might drop to fifty below zero, a channel of open water could suddenly appear. This happened when the ice was caught underneath by a strongly flowing current of water driving in one direction, while above a high wind pushed the exposed ice in the opposite direction. The ice might then be split in two by a channel of open water, with clouds of white, steamy smoke hanging over the break in the ice. These open lanes usually froze over again rather quickly, whenever the wind died down or the sea currents slacked off.

Not only did Allan's iceberg move at its own pace through the surrounding ice, but whole fields of ice were constantly on the move, sometimes crashing into each other, or against the ice cliffs that marked the shores of solid land. Nor was the ice always smooth and level. The constant driving of wind and ocean currents forced it into jumbled masses of ice boulders, of ice ridges and ice valleys, and it was often very difficult indeed to make any progress over the frozen sea.

For that reason Allan did not consider leaving the *Anne Forbes* during the winter months. He would wait for that time between the arrival of daylight again in February, and the breakup of the sea ice in late June or early July. That would be the best time to try and reach land. There would be some daylight to travel by, the ice would still be frozen enough to hike over, and he should reach land just about when the whaling ships would be showing up on their annual run.

In the meantime he tried to fill the long hours of constant darkness as best he could. He often thought of home, of his sisters and mother and especially of his girlfriend Nancy. In a curious way it was because of Nancy that he found himself in his present situation.

All he could have hoped to be at Craigie's, after working for ten or fifteen years, was a tailor. And that did not satisfy him, for he had fallen deeply in love with Nancy and planned to marry her. And he wanted to offer her a better future than just being the wife of an ordinary tailor. So he looked around for a job with more promising prospects. And because his way home took him down to the harbor, he began to make friends with some of the lads who worked the fishing boats. One day he heard that Master Ian MacLoud needed a crew hand. A week later he was getting his sea legs on the herring trawler, *Queen of Argyle*.

The fishing work was cold and dirty, the hours were long, but he made more than twice as much as he made at Craigie's. And if he smelled of fish most of the time, at least it was clean, healthy, outdoor work. Whereas tailors, who worked indoors all the time, squatting over their cloth, were notorious for dying from tuberculosis, the tailor's disease.

Although most of his money went to his mother to help out at home, he always had a little left over to drop in at the drapery shop and spend half an hour buying a length of ribbon or a swatch of velvet for one of his sisters. And naturally he always waited for Nancy to serve him. In fact, he bought so many penny pieces of velvet for his mother and sisters that the other girls in MacLean's Drapery Shop used to jokingly call out to Nancy every time he showed up, "Here comes your Velvet Lad!"

His courtship of Nancy went from silent admiration when they both swept their sidewalks at the same time, through shy conversations when he made his penny purchases in the shop, to Sunday walks on Union Street with her by his side. He found out that Nancy had been born in Edinburgh and moved to Aberdeen when she was a child. Like Allan she was fatherless, though she had many aunts and uncles. As it turned out, Master Duff was a friend of her family too. Aberdeen was a small seaport and nearly everyone knew everyone else. And one day, while sitting on the harbor seawall, she confessed to Allan with many giggles that Master Duff warned her to stay away from "that Gordon lad." Imitating the master's frown and pinched expression, she said, "Have nothing to do with him. Nothing but the wind whistling in one ear and out the other ever disturbs anything inside that great empty barn he carts around on top of his shoulders." And when she told him, he felt a fierce anger and made a promise to himself that one day he would prove the master wrong and set the whole town of Aberdeen on its ear with a tale that would leave everyone talking about him for years. In the meantime he had better stop daydreaming and see about getting something to eat for himself and his hungry pet.

After his meal he reluctantly decided to brave the freezing cold outside and pay the ice mountain a visit. Although there was now constant near-darkness with the sun no longer visible, there were still occasional days and nights of cloudless weather with clear bright moonlight. During these moonlit periods, Allan often went to his cave at the top of the iceberg to see if he could spot any land. He still kept the ice cave supplied all through the winter with frozen meat, with coal and extra clothes. While the *Anne Forbes* was in little danger from ordinary pack ice, Allan never knew when another iceberg, driven by the wind, might crash through the sea ice and into his vessel. He had spotted hundreds of these bergs, both in open water and trapped in the ice. If anything did happen to the *Anne Forbes*, he wanted to be able to take refuge in his iceberg home.

He loaded his fowling piece and called to Nancy. The full moon, reflecting off the snow and ice, made it almost as bright as normal daylight. When Allan finally reached the top of his ice peak, he was in for a pleasant surprise. The air was still, and without a hint of any wind. The extraordinary brightness of the moonlight, together with the stillness of the air, combined to offer greater winter visibility than he had ever seen before. In fact, off about twenty miles or so to the east, there appeared a high jagged ridge on the horizon line. Allan was almost sure that the ridge was the ice-covered cliff of some body of land. Of course the promise of land that far away meant little to Allan. By now he was well aware that his ice island, or indeed the whole ice field, could drift miles away from the land in a day or two. And of course winter, with its scarcity of game, was no time to strike out for a place that, even if he reached it, could prove far more dangerous than his ice island. At least where he was he had a good supply of food.

While Allan was looking around the horizon, marveling how bright and peaceful and still everything was, the silence was ripped apart by the unmistakable crack of a gunshot. Indeed some of the sounds that the ice made when it was under pressure from the sea or the wind resembled the firing of a gun, but on this particular occasion the air was so still, there was so little noise of any kind from the ice, that Allan decided the report he heard could well be a gunshot. He lifted his own fowling piece and fired. For a minute he waited, his heart in his mouth. If there was anyone out there, they should hear his signal and answer him.

"Crack!"

Again the report came. With trembling fingers Allan spilled powder onto the pan of his fowling piece. He would try one more shot to make sure. He touched off another round and this time, when his shot was answered, he was able to make a rough guess where the sound was coming from. Someone was out there on the ice field, about halfway between the iceberg and the ridge of land some twenty miles away.

Allan knew there was no time to be lost if he was to find whoever else was out there on the frozen ice. His first thought was that another whaling ship had been trapped for the winter and a hunting party of the crew had been sent out on the sea ice to try and shoot some polar bears for meat.

Working as fast as he could in the sub-zero cold, he filled his lamp with whale oil and set it out on the observation platform. It would burn for hours and was not likely to go out in the still windless air. In case he had to return to the iceberg, and missed his outgoing tracks, he would have a light to guide him back. For Allan intended to find whoever was out there on the ice.

He hurried down to the *Anne Forbes* and woke up Nancy, who had been sleeping for the past two days.

"C'mon girl, that's a good lassie," he urged,

blowing tobacco smoke into her face. As usual when Nancy woke from a deep sleep, it took her a little while to become fully conscious.

In between nagging and nudging his pet, Allan stocked up on extra gunpowder and shot, packed knapsacks full of food for himself and Nancy, and took along a full bottle of rum.

He finally got Nancy to her feet and the knapsack tied to her back. Urging his pet in front of him, he left the *Anne Forbes*. Then he sealed shut the cabin window from the outside with blocks of snow that he packed into the opening.

When he had gone about a dozen paces, he stopped and turned around for a last look. The black belly of the *Anne Forbes* seemed to lie on the ice like the carcass of a stranded whale.

"Well, Nancy, I pray that's the last we'll ever see of the ice prison that has held us for the past year. Now, in God's name, let us go forward and find whoever is out there."

Although it was very cold, there was almost no wind, which meant that leads of water were not likely to open up and block his way, or force him to make a long detour. Walking in what he judged to be the right direction, he paused every once in a while to carefully search the frozen seas for any signs of life. He walked for hours in the moonlight, until he guessed that he had covered something like ten or twelve miles. And although he often stopped and listened for the sound of voices, for the barking of dogs, for another gunshot — he heard nothing.

The land he had earlier seen from the iceberg was getting closer and closer. At one point when Allan stopped to rest for a moment, Nancy left him and went ranging far off to his right. He was tempted to call her back but decided against it. In fact, he thought, it might not be a bad idea to follow her, perhaps she might lead him to something.

And half an hour later she did. He caught up with her and found her halted at the tracks of men and dogs and sleds, obviously a large hunting party of Eskimos. They could not be stranded whalers, Allan decided, or they would not have dogs and sleds with them.

Allan carefully examined the tracks. The party had halted for a while, perhaps for a rest or to have something to eat. There were boot tracks all over, and in several places yellow patches on the ice from dog urine. It took him a little while of tracking around, going ahead and going back, but he finally figured out that the sleds were heading for land not back out on to the sea ice.

"C'mon Nancy!" he cried out. "We'll soon be with friends!" He felt a great burst of hope.

All he had to do was follow the tracks until he caught up with the sleds. Then his long imprisonment would be over.

The land was now only three or four miles away and surely the party would stop to rest for a while when they reached the shore. With any luck he might spot the sleds and dogs somewhere ahead of him.

Nancy again left him, running on and following the tracks. For a while Allan tried to keep up with her. He was afraid that she would overtake the strangers and that they would shoot her on sight, not knowing that she was a tame bear. But Allan was now getting tired and was forced to halt for another rest. He squinted his eyes, trying to pick out Nancy ahead of him. What he saw made him close his eyes and shake his head. Now he could see *two* Nancys, standing up in front of the tumbled ridge of ice boulders that marked the shore of the land.

Once again he closed his eyes, wondering if his eyesight was playing tricks on him. He looked again and this time made out at least four polar bears in a band. He watched them and noticed that they were now all standing up and looking in his direction.

He squatted down and remained still for minutes, hoping the bears would think he was just a block of ice. But polar bears have an excellent sense of smell. A rotting seal, or whale carcass, for example, will draw them from many miles around.

As soon as the bears caught Allan's scent, they dropped to all fours and came charging out in a wave to meet him.

When Allan saw them coming he jumped to his feet, turned around, and ran for his life.

11

As Allan fled across the ice, he realized the great danger he was in. Polar bears have no natural enemies in the Arctic and therefore have no fear of any living thing, including people. They can outrun a man and easily kill one.

Although Allan had his shotgun with him, and the carving knife in one of his knapsacks, he knew that he could not stand up long against a band of these animals. He might kill one, but the others would swiftly tear him to pieces. His only chance was to keep running and hope that the bears would tire of chasing him. Fortunately he had a good start, at least half a mile.

After he had been running for about twenty minutes, expecting to be overtaken at any moment, he glanced back to check on his pursuers. He noticed then that only two bears were still following him. Exhausted and out of breath, he finally stopped, took the carving knife out of his knapsack, and got his shotgun ready. He took off his two packs and set them on the ice. If he had to use his knife, he did not want the knapsacks getting in the way. Then he sat down on the large sack and waited, ready to sell his life as dearly as possible.

When the bears drew within range, Allan recognized one of them as Nancy. The other was evidently a huge male, as it was twice Nancy's size. Allan felt the first ray of hope. Now he had only one bear to deal with. Then a new and horrible worry hit him. Having met others of her own kind, would Nancy now follow her natural bear instincts and attack him? Or would she remember their close friendship and leave him alone?

As the two bears approached, Allan stood up and made ready to defend himself. Pushing a knapsack out of the way with his foot, he suddenly got an idea. He left the two knapsacks there behind him on the ice and once again began to run. He had not gone far, perhaps a hundred yards, when he was forced to stop. He was still so exhausted that he easily ran out of breath. He turned around, crouched down, and watched the animals come loping toward him over the ice. They reached the pair of knapsacks and stopped. The large bear stood up on his hind legs and once again Allan felt that balloon of fear start to grow inside his stomach. The animal was huge. The bear dropped to all fours again and within minutes the knapsacks were torn apart and both animals were feeding on chunks of whale meat. Still tired and needing a rest, Allan waited. It would take the bears a little while to finish off the food. If the big bear still wanted to chase him, Allan thought, then at least he would have a chance to catch his breath and steady himself for a clear shot at the animal when it charged. He knew he would have time for only one shot. It took too long to reload the old-fashioned fowling piece.

The big bear went snuffling around the torn pieces of canvas, pawing them back and forth. Allan watched a bottle of rum go skidding across the ice to crash into an ice boulder and fly into pieces. The bear brought a piece of canvas to its mouth with one paw and angrily ripped it in two with its teeth. Then the animal stood on his hind legs and stared ahead to where Allan was waiting.

Allan's courage almost failed him. The bear was at least two feet taller than he was and probably weighed over half a ton, or five times more than Allan. Just then Nancy gave one of her whinnying sounds and moved away. The big bear turned in her direction with a questioning grunt. Nancy whinnied again, and again she moved away across the ice. The male bear dropped to all fours and began to follow her.

Allan watched both animals travel away from him until they were lost to view. Was Nancy trying to lure the other bear away from her master? Or had she completely forgotten about Allan in her joy at finding other animals just like herself? Allan couldn't tell, but at least he was out of danger for a little while longer. And although he had grown to love Nancy, he now hoped that she would not return to him, that she would make a new, more natural life with the other bear.

Allan decided to head back to the *Anne Forbes*. He no longer had any food. He was hungry and thirsty and worn out from his march. In his present condition he had little or no chance to catch up with the sled and dog team somewhere ahead of him. And then there were those bears hunting through the shore ice — how was he to get past them? The presence of so many bears surprised him. He had thought that polar bears hibernated all through the winter, but evidently he was wrong. In the spring the bears would probably be less dangerous and would probably be out on the ice floes hunting seals.

As Allan began his return to the *Anne Forbes*, he realized with dismay that he had lost his tracks! He ranged far out to his right, came back, then moved to his left. Finally he found Nancy's paw marks and his own boot-prints, and felt a great sense of relief. All he had to do now was backtrack until he reached the ship.

Allan slung the fowling piece across his back and started the long hike home. For an hour or so he trudged along, growing more and more tired, more and more sleepy. He badly wanted to lie down on the ice and take a little nap. He was now well into his second straight day without any sleep. Allan was not afraid of freezing to death. He was warmly dressed against the cold, and he knew that if he burrowed into the loose snow on the pro-tected side of an ice block, he would be all right. He could always make a snow tunnel, crawl in, and rely on his body heat to keep him warm. After all, he had slept inside a solid block of ice on his iceberg, with only a piece of canvas to keep out the wind.

What worried Allan more than anything else was losing the trail. It was hard enough to pick out in the moonlight as it was. But with his eyes constantly closing, he was afraid of following a false trail and getting lost. On the other hand, he did not dare to make a snow cave, crawl inside, and go to sleep for a couple of hours. The weather might change and a fresh fall of snow cover up his old tracks. Or a wind might spring up and blow snow over them.

But he had to rest, for a little while at least. He placed the butt of his fowling piece on the trail and sat down on a large chunk of ice. Crossing his hands on the muzzle of the gun, he bowed his head and rested his weight on his hands. As soon as he dropped off to sleep, his body relaxed and he fell forward or sideways and woke up. He would then repeat the whole thing until he had managed three or four five-minute rests.

Feeling somewhat fresher, he got to his feet and trudged on. Every hour or so, he would stop for half a dozen catnaps on his gun. It was funny the way things changed, he thought. Only a few hours before he couldn't wait to leave the *Anne Forbes*. Now he couldn't wait to get back to the ship.

It was between catnaps that he heard the sound of some animal coming up on his tracks. Quickly he snatched up the fowling piece and waited. It looked like a bear again, he thought. While the animal was still some distance away, Allan recognized Nancy. Soon she came up to him. Allan was overjoyed and hugged her.

"Nancy! Nancy! My bonny lass! You've come back!"

Nancy lay down at his feet and tried to lick Allan's hand.

"Nancy, wee pet, what's wrong?" Allan asked.

Nancy groveled, as though she had done something wrong.

"Nancy, Nancy, what is it? What's the matter? Ah sure what difference does it make? You're back, thank God."

Now they could easily make it to the *Anne Forbes*, Allan thought. Even if he were to fall asleep, he could rely on Nancy to wake him up. And should he lose their outgoing tracks, he had no doubt that Nancy's sense of smell would lead them back to the cabin of the *Anne Forbes*. In his high spirits he commanded Nancy, "Walk!"

Nancy got up on her hind legs and Allan linked arms with her. "And now madam, I request the honor of walking you home."

Nancy gave a clumsy waddle forward. Just then Allan heard a half bark, half snuffle behind him. He wheeled around to find a tall white column blocking the moonlight.

There, a few feet away, towered the male polar bear!

12

Nancy rushed back to meet the big bear, but the huge animal batted her out of the way with a cuff of his paw. This time the bear did not intend to be led astray. He dropped to all fours and advanced on Allan.

Allan panicked and ran. Earlier, when the two bears first approached him, he had kept his nerve, but he had time then to steady himself, to tell himself that it would do no good to run. This time, however, Allan was not ready for the meeting. The sight of the huge bear, appearing out of nowhere, had frightened him so badly that he could not think. And just when he was sure that he was safe!

As he ran he spotted two large chunks of ice ahead of him. The pieces of ice were leaning against each other and at the bottom there was a small arch of open space. If he could get in between the ice blocks, Allan thought, maybe the bear would leave him alone.

He was still a good fifty feet from his goal

when a huge hand came out of nowhere, clapped him on the back, and sent him sprawling to the ice. He landed on his hands and knees and rolled over, just in time to receive the weight of the huge bear. The animal was now straddling him. Allan tried to pull the carving knife out of his belt but he was unable to reach around to his left hip.

Allan felt the animal's hot breath on his face. He could even smell the whale meat the bear had earlier eaten. For several moments the bear did not seem to know what to do with his captive. He gave Allan a horrible open-mouthed snarl, then raised his head and looked all around, as though to tell any other bears, "This one is mine."

The bear lowered his head again, just as Allan managed to wriggle one arm free. He punched upward, his fist landing on the bear's nose. The animal's head reared upward in surprise, then the great black mouth chomped down on Allan's arm, just above the elbow. The bear's teeth made a deep and terrible wound and Allan began to pass out. He dimly heard Nancy whimper and he had a last minute idea.

"Seize it!" Allan cried with all his strength, using the command he had taught Nancy when he wanted her to bring him something. Then he lost consciousness.

He came to very quickly, perhaps half a minute later, to find that the bear was no longer pinning him down. Nancy had seized the larger animal by the back of the neck, and the male was bellowing angrily, spinning around, trying to get loose from his attacker.

Allan managed to get to his feet and locate his fowling piece. He checked to make sure that the powder was still dry. His left arm was useless and he doubted if he could even hold the gun steady. But he cradled the gun under his right arm and advanced on the two animals. Strangely enough he no longer felt afraid, only angry. He needed both his arms, and that stupid bear had mangled one of them.

The big male was trying to pin Nancy to the ice. Nancy managed to wriggle free at the last minute but the male grabbed her in his powerful forearms. One hind leg doubled up as the bear tried to rip Nancy's belly with his long hind claws. Nancy squirmed and wriggled but the big bear held on. Allan advanced and circled the two struggling animals, trying to find an opening. He was very afraid that he might shoot Nancy by mistake. At last he was able to lift the gun with his right hand and prop the muzzle against one of the bear's ears. He steadied himself, then fired. The recoil knocked him to the ice.

The load of shot ripped away part of the

bear's head but the huge animal continued to claw at Nancy, holding her fast within his forepaws. Both bears rolled over and Allan was afraid that Nancy might yet be killed by the larger animal. Allan got to his feet. With his useless arm he doubted if he could prime and load the fowling piece, so he drew his carving knife and fell on the big bear. He stabbed again and again, in a frenzy, until the large bear, Nancy, and himself were covered with blood. It was hard to believe how long the big bear held on to life.

Nancy finally managed to free herself from the weakening grasp of the male. She came over and lay down at Allan's feet.

Allan knelt down on the ice, put his good arm around her neck and said, "Good lass! Good lass!" Then he passed out.

He was awakened by Nancy's tongue on his face. Allan shook his head. His arm was paining him and he felt dizzy. His shirt and jacket were soaked with blood and it was obvious that he had bled a good deal. He looked over at the huge male. Incredibly, despite a dozen wounds, the animal was still alive. Now and again it bellowed pitifully. Indeed at one point the bear actually got to all fours and scrabbled away a dozen yards before it collapsed.

Finally the animal was dead. Allan thought briefly of skinning it for its fur but he was exhausted and he doubted if he had enough strength to do the job, not to mention dragging the heavy skin back to the *Anne Forbes*. He also thought of coming back in a few days, when he felt stronger, but by then the Arctic foxes would have eaten everything.

He rested for a while on the bloodstained ice before he and Nancy began the long walk home. Fortunately the weather stayed clear and there were no strong winds to cover their outgoing tracks with drifting snows. But the journey soon turned into a nightmare. He often found himself stretched on the ice, so weak he was unable to move. Several times he and Nancy curled up for a nap in the protection of an ice ridge. For a long time Allan did not know where he was going. He had lost his tracks. But again Nancy saved him. She seemed to always know where they were. All Allan knew was that it was very cold, he was very weak, and they had lost their way. At times he was actually raving and imagined he was walking around the Albert Basin, where the fishing boats docked in Aberdeen. He held long wild conversations with the other Nancy, with his sisters and his mother, and once even carried on a long, loud argument with Master Duff.

Through it all Nancy remained by his side. When he fell to the ice, unable to move another step, Nancy lay down beside him and kept him warm. When he passed out completely, she licked his face to bring him to again. When he tried to go the wrong way, she whimpered and nudged him in the right direction.

Finally he fell for the last time, absolutely unable to move another inch. He had stumbled into some sort of hole where he was well protected from the wind. All he wanted to do was curl up and sleep forever. He pushed the fowling piece away from him. Sleep, oh he wanted to go to sleep for a week and then wake up in his loft back home in Aberdeen, with the smell of new baked bread teasing his nose, the song of his mother's voice filling the kitchen below.

But Nancy wouldn't let him go to sleep. In fact she was acting very strangely, digging in the snow. What kind of hole was she digging, Allan asked himself. It was all very queer, and his mother would come upstairs in a minute to explain everything and to tell him that breakfast was ready. Then he had to go and visit the fortuneteller and let her know that she was wrong. No fair lady had ever turned up to save his life.

He closed his eyes and dropped off, but Nancy would not let him sleep. She kept taking his good hand in her mouth and tugging, trying to waken him.

"Go away," he groaned. "Leave me alone,

lass. I can't do it. I don't have the strength to even get up."

But Nancy would not stop her moans and whimpers. At last Allan opened his eyes to yell at her. But instead he found himself looking at a square dark hole a few yards in front of his feet.

"What's this, wee pet?" he asked. Then suddenly he knew. He was looking at the cabin window of the *Anne Forbes!*

13

Somehow Allan got through the hole and into the cabin. The knowledge that he was home revived him somewhat and he covered the window with the iron grate and canvas frame. Then he lit a fire. As soon as he had eaten some meat and biscuits and fed Nancy, he scraped hoarfrost off the wall and into a copper pot and put the pot on the fire. After that he took off his upper clothes to examine his wound. He cleaned the torn flesh as best he could with a rag soaked in water, then poured rum over the wound to kill any germs. Finally, from one of the captain's nightshirts, he made a rough bandage and sling for his arm.

When he was all through treating his own bite, he examined Nancy and discovered that she had received half a dozen wounds, fortunately none of them as serious as his own. Her heavy fur had saved her from the worst of the larger bear's bites and clawings. Allan tried to clean Nancy's bites and claw wounds as best he could, pouring a little rum and water on each place where the larger bear's teeth or claws had broken through the skin. After that Nancy curled up on the cabin floor and went to sleep. Allan filled a cup of rum, lit his pipe, took out the Bible, and read several pages in thanksgiving for his miraculous escape.

And the biggest miracle of all, he thought, was that his pet bear had saved his life not once, but half a dozen times. He would never have made it back to the *Anne Forbes* without her. Only for her timely attack, he would have been killed by the male bear. Not only did Nancy refuse to desert him, but she kept him going in the right direction when he could no longer tell left from right, or up from down. Surely God, or Divine Providence, was keeping a special eye on him. How else could he explain one polar bear fighting another polar bear to save his life.

Utterly tired, Allan gave Nancy a goodnight pat on the rump and climbed into his sleeping closet. Closing the door on the inside, he burrowed down under the covers. Between the rum and his heavy bedclothes, a delicious warmth soon began to steal over his body. He would beat the Arctic yet, he vowed. If it couldn't kill him on this last trip, it would never defeat him. Some day he would swagger along Albert Quay, just like that sailor he once saw, with a gaudy parrot perched on his shoulder and a great gold ring dangling from his ear. "There he goes," the other sailors would say with admiration in their voices, "Iceberg Gordon who survived two years on an ice floe in the Arctic." And thinking such optimistic thoughts, Allan fell asleep.

For the next week he and Nancy did little except sleep and eat and get their strength back. They were worn out from their ordeals and wounds. Although Allan's arm was still painful, the wound healed rapidly in the clear germ-free air of the Arctic. Within a couple of weeks the bite wound had pulled together, and although there was to be some stiffness there for months, he was soon able to use the arm almost as vigorously as ever.

After he was thoroughly rested, Allan again began making plans to leave the *Anne Forbes* as soon as the sun put in an appearance in the south. This time, however, he would be better prepared. After the last trip he was no longer afraid to travel in the dark. Even on overcast days and nights there was always a certain amount of light. Although the stars might be hidden, some of their light still reached the ground where it was picked up and reflected by the snow crystals and bare ice. The only things that cut visibility down to nothing were the dense fogs or heavy snowstorms. And he would simply have to take his chances on those.

Although the time passed slowly now that the sun was completely absent from the heavens, Allan managed to keep busy. He lined the inside of the walls of the cabin with carpet to keep out the cold, a job that took him a couple of weeks of careful cutting and fitting and nailing. He took the mast and sail from his raft and stored them in one of the holds, then tied the raft itself to the keel of the *Anne Forbes* with half a dozen lines.

One day he noticed that the ceiling had a bad sag to it. Having originally been the floor of the cabin, the ceiling had not been built to take the tremendous weight of whale blubber and oil that now rested on top of it. It took him almost a week to cut half a dozen thick oak posts from one of the holds and use them as props for the ceiling over his head.

When these things were done, he began to lay careful plans for the spring. This time he intended to have everything thought out in advance, to have everything he needed with him, to be ready for any emergency. He had all winter to get ready for the trip, and if he didn't make the proper plans, if he didn't use his brains, then he had no one to blame but himself.

His old tailoring skills were put to good use as he spent days making new knapsacks out of sailcloth to replace the ones he had lost. He even made a knapsack for Nancy's back and tried it on her to make sure that it fitted properly. And remembering his fear that Nancy might be shot by hunters, he made a collar and leash for her. He also made a muzzle out of rope. If they ran across a dog team, Allan did not want Nancy trying to bite the smaller animals.

And naturally Allan spent a lot of time thinking of his home in Aberdeen. He especially remembered his decision to sign on the *Anne Forbes*. It had caused a great argument between him and Nancy. That afternoon his trawler had docked at the fishing quay and he had helped unload the day's catch. Then he hurried through the streets, intending to go home, change out of his dirty work clothes and return to Nancy's shop in time to walk her home from work.

As he rounded the corner of Market and Guild streets he bumped into a French sailor who was lost and looking for his ship, the *Jean Christophe*. Allan conducted the sailor back to the docks, and the latter insisted that Allan come on board his ship. Allan did so and was presented with a pound or so of large purple grapes as a gift.

Bearing his grapes in a paper bag, Allan hurried on home. Grapes were a rare imported delicacy in Aberdeen and only showed up in the homes of the rich. Indeed there were many poor people who had never even seen a grape, let alone tasted one. Allan gave half the grapes to his mother and sisters and saved the rest for Nancy. He made it to Maclean's just in time to catch Nancy leaving the shop on her way home.

He fell in beside her and after a few words of greeting, said, "Love, I've made up my mind. I'm going to sign up on the *Anne Forbes*."

Nancy halted to turn around and face him. "A whaling ship?"

"Yes."

"Oh, Allan, why? Whaling is so dangerous. You know how many whalers have been lost."

"Oh, not that many." He caught Nancy by the hand. "Look, wee love, I'll never be able to offer you what you deserve until I have my own fishing trawler. Until then I'll always be laboring for someone else for a few shillings a day."

"But whaling? Aberdeen is full of crippled whalers, and whaler's widows."

"Aye, right enough it's a dangerous trade but I won't be at it long. Two or three voyages, six at the most, and I'll have enough money to buy my own trawler."

"And Allan how long will you be gone? All summer? Until Christmas?"

"We leave next month, the tenth of March. And we should be back by the end of September."

"If you come back at all," Nancy said gloomily.

"Oh, I'll be back."

"Well, you needn't think I'm going to sit around and wait forever for you."

"Ah, wee love, three or four trips is all I need. A lad was telling me the other day that after two voyages I can become a harpooner. They're the kings of the whaling trade and make more than anyone else. It's been known for a harpooner to retire after one good trip."

"Aye," Nancy said darkly. "They've been known to be pulled down by a whale, too."

"Ah now, wee love, sure there's danger in everything." They were standing in front of an ironmonger's store. Allan was leaning back against the store window, through which could be seen a brand new plow, and an assortment of shovels and pitchforks and other farm tools. He set the bag of grapes on the outside wooden ledge of the window and put both arms around Nancy's waist. "Wee dear, just a trip or two to get me started. And although I'll be away all summer, I'll be around all winter. You know how you worry about me fishing during the winter storms."

She pushed Allan's arms away. "Oh, do what you like, you will anyway." She wriggled out of his grip and hurried off.

"Ach, wait a minute, Nancy," Allan called after her as he hurried to catch up. He pleaded with her all the way home, pointing out that he was going whaling only because he loved her and wanted to offer her a better future than just being the wife of an ordinary fisherman. Also he wanted to be his own boss, own his own boat, and whaling was the only quick path to money for someone like him. Could she not understand that?

And it was only standing outside her door that he remembered the grapes. He had left them at the ironmonger's store!

"I'm away," he suddenly cried out. "I've forgotten the grapes!"

"The grapes?" Nancy echoed.

"Aye, I had a bag of grapes for you."

He sped off into the darkness and when he reached the ironmonger's he found the grapes gone. He slumped against the window and mentally kicked himself. "Idiot!" he called aloud. Someone had noticed the bag sitting there and had made off with a lovely bunch of grapes.

And ever after that night, from then until the day he sailed on the *Anne Forbes*, Allan promised Nancy that to make up for the lost grapes he would bring her back a bunch of grapes from Vinland.

He leaned forward and placed another coal on the fire. He was a long way now from Aberdeen, and poor Nancy must have given him up for dead long ago. Especially when the second summer passed without any word of the *Anne Forbes*. People would know that the ship had gone down with no hope of any survivors.

"Ah, Nancy, Nancy, will I ever see you again?" Allan called out.

His pet bear whimpered and came over to lay her head on his knees. He scratched her forehead. "Aye, you're the only one I have left now, you poor dumb brute."

And so Allan waited out the winter and planned for spring. By now he had a rough idea of where he was. The *Anne Forbes* had been north and east of Greenland when she struck the iceberg. For the first few weeks after that, the berg, caught by a strong current, had drifted north. After that, with the onset of the Arctic night, Allan had no idea of where he was going. But when spring came again and lengthened into summer, and he sighted land on two occasions, he guessed that the berg had somehow rounded the southern tip of Greenland and made its way north to Baffin Bay or Davis Strait, which was another good reason to leave the berg by early spring.

If the iceberg were in Davis Strait, it might well be carried south and by the end of the summer be out in the open Atlantic, rapidly melting in the warmer waters of the Gulf Stream.

So Allan kept busy with his plans, getting his equipment ready, making extra clothing, taking frequent trips with Nancy to his ice peak on moonlit days and nights to keep watch. And what he longed to see, even more than land or a ship's sail, was the return of the sun.

14

The winter proved to be even colder and
stormier than the year before. On one occasion
Allan was stuck inside the cabin for a full
week because of a blizzard. Almost every time
he went outside he had to dig his way through
the snow tunnel. He thought of making a covering of some kind for the trench, a makeshift
roof, but decided against it. The snow in the
tunnel helped to keep the cabin warm. The
extra warmth was well worth the digging it
took whenever he wanted to go outside.

As the Arctic night wore on, Allan realized
that this would have to be his last winter on
the *Anne Forbes*. For one thing he was running low on coal. He still had a dozen bucket-
fuls on the peak of the iceberg, but he wanted
to save those in case something happened to
the *Anne Forbes*. He could always burn the
timbers of the ship itself if he had to. Although it was hard work to hack at the tough

oak with his hatchet, he would do it if it became necessary. But that would actually be burning his house, only to be tried if all else failed.

One day, or rather night, since the sun had not yet put in an appearance, Allan climbed his ice peak and saw, on the southern horizon, a fan-shaped patch of sky colored red and gold. Although the sun was still hidden, Allan knew that it would not be long until daylight returned once more to the Arctic. The light would last a little longer each day until early May, when the sun would not set at all. Then there would be no darkness but twenty-four hours of daylight every day. Whistling, Allan went back to the *Anne Forbes* and began to make ready. The next day the rim of the sun appeared, a very bright red edge peeking up over the horizon. Some weeks later the sun had climbed high enough into the sky to provide a couple of hours of daylight every day.

By the end of March, Allan was ready to leave the *Anne Forbes*. He had already spent days filling the cave on his ice peak with frozen whale meat, with extra clothing, with shavings and coal for a fire. Almost everything he did not intend to take with him he brought to his summer home on the iceberg peak. He was afraid that the *Anne Forbes* might disappear, crushed beneath the leading edge of another ice field, or sunk in the freezing water because the ledge she was resting on had broken off. Allan had no intention of returning to his ice island, but if another misfortune occurred, another meeting with polar bears, or an open channel of water that he could not cross, he wanted to be able to come back and be sure that he could survive through the summer on the iceberg. There would still be the chance of a whaling ship spotting his signal flag. Or the berg might come close enough to land that his raft could ferry him across. One thing he was sure of, he had no intention of spending a third winter on the iceberg!

And so, a few hours before sunrise one morning, Allan was outside blocking the entrance to the *Anne Forbes* with chunks of ice. He spent an hour filling in the entrance tunnel so that wild animals, especially bears, would not be able to break in.

Then he got into his two knapsacks, one on his chest and one on his back. Calling Nancy, he strapped her into her knapsack and put the collar around her neck.

"Well, are we ready?" he asked.

Nancy reared up on her hind legs, ready to go for a Sunday stroll.

"Say good-bye to our home," Allan ordered.

He picked up his fowling piece, took a long

last look at the rounded hump of the *Anne Forbes*, then turned his back on the ship and looked off to the east where a light patch in the sky showed that the sun would soon be rising. Then he and Nancy left the iceberg for the bleak and empty ice fields that surrounded them.

Using the sun when it was visible, Allan set a course west by southwest. If he were in Baffin Bay or Davis Strait, he knew land lay in that direction. Even if he were on the other side of Greenland, somewhere off the eastern coast, such a course would take him to the mainland instead of out into the open ocean. He set the course mainly to the south because he had no way, other than guessing direction from the position of the sun, to determine the exact points of the compass. And if he were going to make any mistakes in direction, he wanted those mistakes to lead him to the south. He had had enough of the north!

Allan was prepared to travel for days, perhaps even weeks, before he met anyone. After twelve hours of steady marching, he made a brief camp in a sheltered spot on the windward side of an upthrust ridge of ice. Here he took some meat and a couple of biscuits out of his pack. He also took out a piece of whale blubber for Nancy, which the animal swiftly gulped down. With the meat, biscuits, and dried fish in his pack, Allan figured he had enough food to survive at least two weeks. Nancy's pack contained about fifty pounds of whale blubber, which he knew would only last her a couple of days. After that he would count on her catching fish if they came to any open water, or perhaps a careless young seal out on the ice. At least both of them had started out in good shape. For the past month Allan had been fattening himself and Nancy as much as possible ahead of time. Then if they ran short of food they could, like the Eskimos, live off their body fat for a while.

Allan had already traveled through the three hours or so of daylight, but fortunately it was a clear night and the starshine provided plenty of visibility. He rested behind a hummock of ice for half an hour or so, until he felt his limbs beginning to stiffen with the cold. Then he got to his feet and resumed the march.

Two hours later he spotted half a dozen white doglike animals in the distance. They seemed to be circling something on the ground. Allan halted and tied the leash to Nancy's collar. If they were wolves, he wanted no part of them!

He waited, trying to make up his mind what to do. Even if the animals had killed something and he managed to scare them away from the carcass, he had no need of more meat. Both his packs were still full.

As his route would pass close to the animals, Allan decided to keep a sharp eye on the scene as he went by. Cautiously he advanced and had not gone very far when one of the animals spotted him and gave a whinnying bark. The others stopped eating and raised their heads. By now Allan recognized them as the most common scavengers to be found in the polar wastes — white Arctic foxes. No longer afraid, he released Nancy from the leash and marched boldly ahead.

Nancy scampered over the ice to the foxes and the animals scattered. She began to paw at the ice and whimper. The foxes, a safe distance away, sat down and watched her. Now and again one would lift his head and give an angry bark.

"Nancy! Come back. Here girl, come back," Allan called.

But Nancy ignored him, something she hardly ever did. Allan had no intention of going out of his way to discover what had attracted the foxes. Probably they had found the remains of a dead seabird. As far as he could tell there wasn't even the carcass of an animal there. He needed to save his strength for the rest of the march. It wasn't very sensible to make unnecessary detours. He called

Nancy again, and again she refused to come, but instead sat down and whimpered.

For a moment he was tempted to march on and trust that she would eventually follow him. Finally, though, he remembered the last time they had marched out, when Nancy found the tracks of men and dogs. He had better hike over and see what was keeping her.

When he reached the spot, he could hardly believe his eyes! In that vast immensity of ice and cold, of empty horizons, Nancy had managed to find the tracks of men and dogs and sleds. He let out a great shout, then threw his arms around Nancy and kissed her cold black nose. Once more his pet had saved him!

When he could think calmly again, Allan noticed all the blood surrounding a plate-sized hole in the ice. The three or four men had obviously killed a seal, then taken the dead animal along with them. The scent of blood had attracted the foxes, though why the scavengers still hung around he had no idea. Except for some bloodstains there wasn't a shred of the seal to be found. The hunters had obviously thrown the whole animal onto their sled and made off with it. After a slow and careful examination of the tracks, Allan decided that there was only one sled with three or four hunters and six to eight dogs.

With a light heart Allan began to follow the

sled tracks. He had not gone far when he noticed that the foxes had returned to the scene of the killing. Curious, he watched them. They were eating the reddened snow and licking the bloodstained ice to take advantage of every last drop of nourishing blood that had been spilled. At the rate they were going, the foxes would have the place cleaned up in no time. Allan realized then that had he come by a half hour later, the foxes would have already licked up all the evidence and be gone. He could have passed within a few yards of the tracks and never noticed anything out of the ordinary.

Unlike the time he had tried to follow his own tracks back to the *Anne Forbes*, Allan was able to pick out the trail without any difficulty. The hunting party left plenty of evidence, and at one spot he could tell they had stopped for a while because their sled had overturned.

But after an hour on the trail, Allan was forced to halt and make a decision. The wind was springing up, cutting visibility down to a few yards, and blowing snow over the tracks he was trying to follow. If the wind got much worse, there was a good chance that he would lose the trail. It was therefore important to overtake the hunting party before the wind increased, or the weather changed, bringing a fresh fall of snow.

Allan was carrying close to a hundred pounds of food and supplies. He guessed, from the freshness of the seal blood, that the hunters had a couple of hours start on him. If he hoped to catch them, he would have to lighten his load. Already he was close to exhaustion and he had not been on the trail for even twenty-four hours yet.

He halted and struggled out of his chest pack. It contained a variety of whale blubber, salted mutton and venison, and dried fish. Nancy managed to eat the whale blubber, although she wouldn't touch the salted meat. Allan was able to squeeze several slabs of frozen dried fish beneath the straps of his backpack. The rest of the fish he gave to Nancy and she swiftly gobbled them down.

He hated to leave the salted meat behind, but it was more important to overtake the hunting party ahead of him. If he missed the band of hunters, he might starve to death before he found anyone else in those thinly peopled regions.

Allan got to his feet and, his load now much lighter, set out with a firm determination not to stop again until he had caught up with the hunters.

"Lay on MacDuff!" he cried to Nancy, and the two white figures, man and beast, made their slow way across the jumbled plains of ice.

The hours passed. Several times Allan was sure that he spotted land ahead, only to have the high white bluffs melt away into the mist when he drew closer. Once he thought he heard dogs barking, but Nancy paid no attention to the sounds and he decided reluctantly that he was hearing things. Several times he was forced to stop and rest, and once he fell asleep curled up on the ice. But Nancy soon got restless and woke him up with her whimpering and moaning. Painfully Allan got to his feet, picked up the sled tracks, and staggered on.

Once again the daylight came, a wintry sun that surprisingly made it even harder to pick out the tracks. The low slanting rays, coming from behind Allen, bounced off the ice ahead of him and reflected back into his eyes. Worried about snow blindness, Allan took shelter for a hour or so and rested up rather than face into that continual glare.

Almost forty-eight hours after he left the *Anne Forbes* he came to a particularly rough belt of broken ice where huge boulders, some of them twenty feet high, had been piled on top of each other. It was tough picking his way between them, but he had the consolation of knowing it was even harder for the hunters with their loaded sled.

It took an hour to work through the rough

ice before he had fairly smooth ice once more stretching ahead of him, with the twin score-marks of the sled runners plainly to be seen. Although the smooth ice was easier to travel over, it meant that the hunters, aided by the eager dogs, were probably pulling ahead of him, widening the distance between the two parties. So he was not unhappy when he ran across another range of ice hills, even higher than the last girdle of broken ice.

He halted for a moment to survey the ice bluffs ahead of him. He staggered forward another fifty yards, then stopped again. The tops of the ice bluffs were black, swept bare of any snow by the wind. He was looking at the rounded top of a low granite cliff!

Allan staggered ahead and crawled and clawed his way to the top of the bluff. He took the mitten off his right hand and patted and felt the actual rock with his bare fingers to make sure he was really on dry land. Then he knelt down and said a prayer of thanks-giving.

He was free of the sea at last!

15

After a short rest, Allan forced himself to his
feet. Although he was very tired, he was anxious not to miss the hunting party. He called
to Nancy and picked up the tracks again. He
noted that the hunters did not go inland but
seemed to be following the edge of the shore.
Some hours later he ran across a wide circle
of trampled-down snow where the hunters
had obviously rested for a while. He sank to
the ground, throughly discouraged. He had
counted on the fact that a man traveling alone
would surely overtake a loaded sled and dog
team. But somehow he had missed them. Now
well rested, the party had gone on and Allan
was at the end of his strength. His body refused to take another step without some
needed rest. He was even too tired to eat,
though he did melt a few mouthfuls of snow
to ease his thirst.

Sunk down in the snow, Allan felt himself

dropping off to sleep. He knew he should try and find a better shelter, but it was still below freezing and the cliff edge where he now rested was open to the wind. His head dropped to his knees as he crouched in a snow pocket. In a minute, he told himself, just a minute's rest and then he would go on again.

Some time later he was awakened by whimpers from Nancy. He struggled to his feet, swayed upright for a minute, then crashed to the ground. There was no feeling of any kind in his feet and they were obviously frostbitten. Once more forcing himself erect, he used his fowling piece as a staff and stamped his feet up and down until, slowly, some feeling returned to his toes. After a while both feet began to throb with pain. He welcomed the pain, knowing it was a sign that the blood was once more freely circulating in his feet.

Meanwhile Nancy had been digging furiously at the ground. Allan went over to where the animal was pawing at a low mound of snow. The snow had been all trampled and packed down. Together he and Nancy dug down until they came to a layer of rocks. Allan managed to lift aside one of the heavy slabs and underneath it found the frozen body of a seal!

Taking out his carving knife, he hacked and chopped out a piece of seal meat for Nancy and threw it to her. He would have fed her more, but the meat did not belong to him.

Allan covered up the seal carcass and packed the snow tight around the rocks. Then he went to the edge of the low cliff and looked out over the frozen sea ice. He could not see very far in the poor light but there did not seem to be anything moving out there. He retreated to the food mound and sat down for a moment to think. He had to catch some rest before he went on. Sleep perhaps he could do without. With the freezing temperatures he probably would not drop off for more than ten or fifteen minutes at a stretch before the cold got through his clothes and woke him up. But his body, especially the muscles in his legs and thighs, cried out for rest.

Allan began to puzzle over the food cache. Whoever the hunters were, they had been careless in covering up the seal. Polar bears or wolves would make short work of the mound if they happened to run across it. Even the small but clever Arctic fox would eventually find a way to get at the meat. Unless, of course, the hunters meant to leave the meat there for only a short time while they went back to their village to tell others of their kill. But why not bring the seal with them? Or perhaps they had left the meat there to go out hunting again. But if it were seal they were after, wouldn't they head right out on to the sea ice? Instead they seemed to be following the shore. Of course they might be following the shore because the land was a good fifty feet higher than the frozen sea and would offer them better visibility.

Allan was faced with a difficult choice. He could stay where he was, hoping the hunters would soon return for that seal. Or he could once more follow their tracks and hope to overtake them. Either way there were dangers. If he stayed, the weather might change and the hunter's tracks be buried under new snow. Nor could he be sure that someone would soon return for the seal. Suppose something happened to the hunters? Suppose, while crossing a thin patch of ice, the sled and men went through and were drowned? He could wait forever before anyone showed up.

On the other hand, if he decided to follow the tracks, he might not be strong enough, or fresh enough, to overtake the men before his own strength gave out. He might die of starvation on the trail. Or he might lose the tracks entirely. Or the trail might stop at open water, where the hunters had arranged to meet other men with boats, and continue their journey by sea.

But whatever he decided to do, he simply had to take a few hours' rest. He called Nancy and commanded her to lie down. He then took the leash out of his pack, tied one end to Nancy's collar and the other end around his wrist. If the hunters returned, he did not want Nancy getting into a fight with their dogs.

When that was done, Allan lay down on the ground, using Nancy's body as a shelter from the wind. In a few minutes he dropped off, his first true sleep in almost forty-eight hours.

He was wakened several times in the next hour as Nancy tugged on the leash. The Arctic daylight came again and the bear got curious about a large white bird that landed on the ground some twenty yards away. Allan woke up and looked over at the bird. Nancy kept tugging on the leash, wanting to go over and investigate the new arrival, but the bird fortunately took off and Nancy settled down again. Allan was able to go back to sleep.

The next time Nancy woke him she was whimpering. From the way her head was lifted and moving from side to side, Allan knew that she had scented something.

"What is it?"

Again Nancy whimpered.

"Somebody coming?"

Then Allan heard the cries of someone far out on the ice. He got to his feet. Now he could hear the unmistakable barking of a dog.

Quickly he fitted the homemade muzzle over

Nancy's snout. She did not like the muzzle and tried to paw it off her nose and mouth.

"Stop!" Allan ordered.

Nancy whimpered and sat down on the snow.

Allan crept forward to the edge of the cliff and looked down. Now, at the last minute, he had doubts about his meeting with these strangers. Suppose they were savages who might decide to take no chances and kill him on sight? Allan knew little about Eskimos but he had heard all the usual rumors about them from the superstitious sailors of whaling ships. Some Eskimos were supposed to have only one eye in the middle of their foreheads. Others were supposed to dig holes in the snow, crawl in, and go to sleep for the winter. Some sailors of that time even believed that the bodies of Eskimos were covered with scales, which was why the cold had no effect on them! The last rumor probably got started when some sailor saw an Eskimo roll completely over and over in his kayak without seeming to get wet or even cold from the freezing water!

Down below, three men were easing a loaded sled through the jumbled shore ice. The dogs strained and two of the hunters lifted and wrestled the sled through a narrow opening between two ice blocks. For a moment the hunters were lost to view. Then they reappeared with the sled and dogs at the foot of a low cliff. One of the men, seeking a way up the bluff, noticed Allan above. He called to the others and the three hunters gathered in a knot to stare at Allan.

Allan stood up and called down to them. In his excitement at talking to humans again for the first time in nearly two years, he forgot that they would not understand his language.

"Halloo down there! I am from the whaling ship *Anne Forbes* out of Aberdeen. I am shipwrecked, a castaway. My name is Allan Gordon."

One of the hunters shouted something in reply and Allan, still expecting to hear English, thought the man was telling him to wait. At this Allan did a little dance of joy on top of the cliff, throwing his arms up in the air and hopping back and forth from one foot to another. His excitement caught Nancy and she also stood up. Allan held her by the leash and called out, "Have no fear, the poor brute is tame!"

But the three Eskimos were thoroughly frightened now. One yanked a spear from the sled while the other two urged the dogs to turn around. Allan's dance of joy they took to be threatening gestures, and when the bear stood up it only added to their terror. What kind of human traveled with a bear? Nor did they understand a word that Allan had said. They did not recognize his strange dark clothing, none of which was made from sealskin or caribou hide or polar bear fur. Nor did this dark stranger make the usual sign of greeting between Eskimos who did not know each other; hands up at shoulder level, palms facing outward.

It is little wonder that they decided to forget their meat cache and get as far away as possible from that devil up there on the cliff. The Eskimos were no less superstitious than the sailors and wanted nothing to do with the sort of supernatural beings who travel around with polar bears. Eskimos too had their evil spirits, their devils who dwelt in the belly of the earth or high up on glaciers.

Hardly able to believe his eyes, Allan watched the hunters turn the sled around, and heard the cry of one of them urging the dogs back out on the ice. At that moment he fell to his knees and began to weep. To have come so far, to have suffered so much, only to be denied the chance of rescue at the last possible moment.

"Come back!" he cried. "Please come back!"

But his cries were ignored.

16

As Allan, with sinking heart, watched the sled, he noticed that the Eskimo with the spear was walking backwards. The hunter held his weapon at the ready, as though to defend the rear of the sled from attack. Allan remembered then the woman he had frightened the previous summer, and suddenly realized that the hunters were afraid of him.

He had an idea and commanded Nancy, "Down! Lie down like a good girl."

Nancy sat down and Allan rested one hand on top of her head, to show that she was under his control. Then, kneeling there at the edge of the cliff, he began to beg for his life. He lifted his arms as though in prayer and cried out, over and over again, both a prayer to God and an appeal to the hunters, "In the name of Jesus Christ don't leave me here! In the name of Christ Jesus don't abandon me!"

Nancy sat up and lifted her paws, as though she too were begging for help.

The hunter carrying the spear called to his two companions and they stopped the sled. All three Eskimos looked back and up at Allan.

"In the name of Jesus Christ help me!" Allan called.

The leader of the hunters understood several things at once. He realized that the bear was tame, and that if the human on the cliff meant them any harm he would hardly kneel down in an act of surrender. Also Allan's lifted arms looked very much like the Eskimo sign of friendship. And finally, the Eskimo thought he recognized the name *Jesus Christ*. He turned to the others and said something. They shook their heads. The hunter faced towards Allan again, placed his spear upright on the ice and cried out, "Jesu Christus! Jesu Christus!"

Allan called out again, this time using the hunter's Latin pronunciation of the Lord's name. "In the name of Jesu Christus come back!"

Once more the dogs and sled were turned around. Realizing that the hunters were coming back for him, Allan remained kneeling at the cliff edge. He was so overcome with emotion that the tears rolled down his face as he said a prayer of thanks.

Soon the dog team and hunters appeared on the top of the bluff. The dogs were tied up some distance away, so that they could not attack Nancy. And Allan left the muzzle on Nancy's head, so that she could not bite the dogs. He commanded her to lie down and she did so. Then he advanced to meet the Eskimos.

The hunters were very curious about Allan. One of them reached up and pinched Allan's cheek, as though to make sure that he was real. Another hunter gave Allan's thick blonde hair a gentle tug. Allan bore the inspection with patient good humor.

The leader of the group had a face that was all to one side and horribly scarred. His black hair fell in long lank strands and his tiny dark eyes were almost hidden by rolls of fat high on his cheekbones. It was this one who pointed to himself and said, "Intuk!" Then he pointed to the other two: "Ootah! Krickvik!" The other two hunters gave big broad smiles.

"Allan!" Allan said, pointing to himself.

"Allan!" they repeated, then pointed to Nancy and gave her the Eskimo word for bear, *Nanook!*

Next the hunters took seal meat from their provisions in the sled and offered a piece to Allan. He took it and began to chew. Then, by means of sign language, he let them know that he had found their seal and given some of the meat to Nancy. He learned that the Eskimos had another seal carcass on the sled. The seal

Allan found had been their first kill. As he suspected, they had left the carcass there because they did not want to load up the sled until they had gone out on the ice again to see if they could make another kill. They had been successful on their second hunt and had been coming back to pick up their first kill when they ran across Allan.

Allan now realized that if he had rushed on and followed the sled tracks instead of taking a rest at the meat cache, he would have made a big circle of four or five hours hiking, only to come back to where he had started. And he might not have been able to overtake the party, or he might have lost the sled tracks out on the ice.

After a short rest, Intuk got the dogs to their feet again and pulled the sled up to the meat cache. The three hunters loaded the first seal carcass on to the sled and took the knapsacks and shotgun from Allan and stowed them away. Then they called to the dogs and began to make trail. Allan and Nancy followed at the rear of the sled.

After many hours of travel, they halted and built two snowhouse igloos, one for themselves and one for Allan and Nancy. They fed the dogs with raw seal meat and prepared, over a cooking lamp, a sort of fresh seal-meat stew that Allan found delicious, especially the heavy liquid soup that remained. In turn he offered the hunters some dried fish and some whale meat from his knapsack. They recognized both foods immediately. The ship biscuits they found tasty but they had a lot of trouble swallowing the rum and it was obvious that they had never tasted strong drink before. One sip of the liquid was enough and they refused to drink any more.

After another two full days and nights of travel, the party reached a large body of open water where the hunters had left two canoes and a larger boat. The Eskimos put Allan in the bigger boat with both seal carcasses, most of the dogs, the sled, and one of the hunters. The other dogs went into the canoes and snuggled at the feet of their masters. For a while Allan was worried about Nancy. They had to leave her behind on the shore as there was no room for her in the boats. And even had they been able to squeeze her into the larger boat, the dogs would have given her no peace, and travel would have been impossible. However, when Nancy saw the three boats move out from shore, she slid into the water and began to swim after them, determined to follow her master.

The boats were met on the other side of the bay by a dozen women and children. They swiftly surrounded Allan and found him an object of great curiosity. Their interest soon turned to terror when Nancy waddled out of the water and came towards them. The women and children scattered and it was only with difficulty that the Eskimo hunters convinced them that Nancy was harmless.

And so, surrounded by excited women and children, the party made its way along the shore for some miles until they reached a group of caves under a high rock bluff. In front of the cliff stretched a narrow but deep beach of fine pebbles.

Outside the caves they were greeted by a tall old man with white hair and a long white beard. The man gave his name to Allan as Herard and made a motion for Allan to kneel down. Allan did so and the old man put one hand on Allan's head and raised his other hand to heaven. Again Allan caught the words, "Jesu Christus," and guessed that the old man was the tribe's priest and was giving him a sort of blessing.

By signs the old man gave Allan to understand that he was welcome and was not to be afraid. Then Allan was escorted back into the caves by Intuk and given a room for himself and Nancy.

When Intuk left, Allan sat down on the floor and thought about his rescue. It would not be long now until he was on his way home to

Aberdeen. Surely the Eskimos knew about the whaling ships, perhaps they even traded with the whalers? And surely they would take him to where he could join one of the ships? Why in a month, maybe even a week, he might be back with his own people again. Within a couple of months he could be walking into MacLean's Drapery Shop and surprising the life out of Nancy.

Allan took out his pocket Bible and read a couple of pages. Then he left the cave and went to see about getting some food for Nancy. He was in great spirits, positive now that his long ordeal was almost over.

It was just as well that Allan could not see into the future. He was still a long way from home.

17

The hunters who found Allan belonged to a tribe of thirty-one women, ten men, and seven children. Only two of the children were boys. At first Allan thought that he had fallen in with a tribe of Eskimos who had been converted to Christianity. Although their religion was rather primitive and often mixed up with pagan beliefs and customs, they did believe in Jesus Christ, and they used the cross as a symbol to ward off evil spirits and to bring them good luck on a hunt.

While serving on the *Anne Forbes*, Allan had heard that Danish missionaries were in Greenland hoping to convert the Eskimos. But when Allan tried to find out if it was the Danish missionaries who brought Christianity to the tribe, he ran into some puzzling facts. The tribe members, especially Herard, who knew the tribal history back for a very long time, said that the tribe had been Christian for many years, for hundreds of years. Herard knew of no missionaries; no Europeans had ever paid them a visit.

As best he could, Allan questioned them about the whalers. Yes, they had seen the great ships on the seas but they had never gone on board any of the huge vessels, nor had they ever talked to any of the sailors. They were afraid to. They had heard, from another tribe of Eskimos, that the whaleships captured Eskimos and brought them to their own countries to serve as slaves.

Most of this information came in bits and pieces and Allan was never sure if he fully understood what Herard, or Intuk or Ootah, was telling him. Because he did not understand their language, he had to rely on signs, and pictures drawn on the sand of the beach, and imitations with his body, to get his thoughts across. It was all very difficult and some things he was sure he had gotten wrong. For example, he thought that Herard told him that none of the members of the tribe were Eskimos, but had all come to the land where Eskimos lived from a country that was very far to the east, many days sail across the sea. In fact Allan began to suspect that Herard meant that the tribe originally came from Europe. The members of the tribe even seemed to recognize the name *Norway*. But that was impossible. Herard and the others were obviously Eskimo! In order to clear up these mysteries, Allan decided to learn the tribe's language as soon as possible.

The tribe made its home in caves beneath an overhanging cliff. There was a large cave, with many small rooms leading off it. Because the ground at the back of the cliff was permanently frozen, the hunters used small rooms in this part of the cave for storing food. Such rooms were natural refrigerators.

The larger areas at the front of the cave were closed in with walls of caribou skin erected over frames of driftwood and whalebone. In winter the tribe took down the skin tents and made igloos. And just like an igloo, the main entrance to the cave had a long snow tunnel that could be entered only on hands and knees. On very cold nights in winter, the dogs crept into this snow tunnel for warmth.

Nancy soon became a favorite with the tribe, and the children loved to take her fishing. They thought it was great fun to see her slide into the water, come back up with a fish in her mouth and lay it on the ground in front of them. Needless to say she did not give up all her fish but kept one for herself every once in a while. But Nancy had trouble with the dogs, who were often used to hunt polar bears and therefore saw Nancy as an enemy.

Because of the dogs, who slept outside the cave or at the tunnel entrance, Nancy stayed with Allan in one of the rooms inside the cave. Allan soon trained Nancy to pay no attention to the dogs and to avoid them as much as possible. As time passed, the dogs learned to leave Nancy alone. For one thing she could easily kill one of them with a swipe of her paw.

As long as Nancy stayed with the tribe, she and the dogs never became friendly. Strangely enough, the several puppies at the camp had no fear of Nancy and she often played with them. The puppies would growl and tug at her fur and Nancy would tumble them upside down and roll them over on the ground with her paw, yet she never hurt any of them.

As soon as Allan learned a few words of the tribe's language, he began to urge Intuk to make a trip to the *Anne Forbes*. But Allan soon realized that the tribe had more than one master. While Herard was a sort of priest and wise man, when it came to hunting or making any trips away from camp, it was Intuk who led the party. However, Ootah seemed to be the most popular man in camp. Whenever any disputes came up, Ootah was called in to solve them. Inusklik, one of the older women, was the tribe's doctor. She knew what medicines to make for infections, what prayers to say for each sickness. Allan soon became special friends with one of the young hunters, Ireek by name. Ireek was about the same age as Allan, which made it easier to become friends with him.

Allan soon discovered that the men were afraid to make a trip to the *Anne Forbes*. Perhaps they thought that all of Allan's friends were still on the ship and might seize them or do them harm. Perhaps they found it hard to believe that one of those huge ships could simply be abandoned to the ice.

As the days, and then weeks passed, Allan learned more and more of the new language. The more he learned, the harder he worked to get Intuk to search for the *Anne Forbes*. Allan appealed to the women. The canvas of Allan's knapsack and the cloth of his clothing astonished the women, and they found it hard to believe that such materials were made from fibers and did not come from the backs of animals. The women made all the clothing for the tribe and were extremely skilled at the job. They could make sealskin boots that were so tightly sewn as to be absolutely waterproof. They could make jackets and trousers that were coldproof as well as waterproof. But all the materials they used in their clothing came from the skins of animals and birds. Allan let it be known that there was much cloth and canvas on the *Anne Forbes* and this particularly interested the women. It took a long time to make an animal skin into clothing. Every tiny piece of fat had to be carefully scraped off the hide, and then the skin itself had to be chewed and chewed again so that it would be soft enough to bend easily when it was dry. For this reason, a supply of canvas or cloth seemed very desirable to the women.

Then Allan turned to the men. The hunters very much admired Allan's carving knife since they had no metal tools or weapons of any kind. Old Herard did remember his father talking about a wonderful material — iron — that could be used in knives and harpoon and spear points, a material that never wore out. The tribe had no iron of any kind and made all their weapons and tools from whale and walrus and caribou bone. They even made fishing hooks and sewing needles out of bone! So Allan told them there was plenty of iron on the *Anne Forbes*, enough iron to last the tribe for many, many years. But they had to go soon. If they waited much longer, the sea ice would break up and the *Anne Forbes* sink, or drift many miles out of their way.

Finally one day, a month after Allan's arrival, it was decided that Intuk and five other men would take all the healthy dogs and half a dozen sleds and look for the *Anne Forbes*.

It took Allan and the men six days to find the ship, but the trip was well worthwhile. They loaded everything they could onto the sleds — boxes of tobacco and the box of clay pipes; all sorts of weapons like hatchets, lances, javelins, blubber knives, and the long flensing knives used for cutting up the whales; boathhooks; the carpenter's box of tools (which were badly rusted but still usable); the captain's silverware; baskets and buckets and kegs of nails. They took half a dozen pieces of pig iron, part of a supply that had been used for ballast on the ship. They took barrels of meat and what was left of the barrel of rum. Everything was loaded on the sleds — sail canvas from the raft, clothing, carpeting from the cabin, oil lamps, rope, and coal. They loaded one sled with nothing but whale blubber so that they could make a fast run home and not have to stop and hunt seal for themselves and the dogs.

At last all the sleds were loaded and everyone ready for the trip back. Allan turned around for a last look at the ship. For a moment he actually felt homesick for his cabin. The *Anne Forbes* had kept him alive for almost two years, and he knew that he would never see the old wreck again.

"Say good-bye to our old home, Nancy," he ordered his pet.

With a shout, Intuk called to his dogs, and the animals fanned out, leaning into their sealskin traces. Soon half a dozen sleds and several dozen dogs were scattered over the ice. Allan and Nancy had to hurry to keep up.

In three days the men were back at their home camp and everyone was very happy and excited by all the new material the tribe had acquired. They all learned to smoke and went at it with such enthusiasm that in less than a week all the tobacco was gone. However some of the men learned to smoke dried moss and claimed it was even better than tobacco. The women were delighted by the fine slender needles of Allan's housewife kit. Their own needles were made from caribou bone, which steadily wore away and often broke.

The hunters, especially Krickvik, who made the best harpoons, learned to tip all their weapons, their lances and harpoons and caribou-blade knives, with iron points that were well sharpened on a piece of whetstone salvaged from the *Anne Forbes*.

One day Allan took his fowling piece and, with the whole tribe watching, shot a snow ptarmigan, a bird frequently found in the Arctic. The men were more impressed with the noise than anything else. Some thought Allan managed the trick through a sort of magic. Intuk was actually disappointed when he found out that Allan's gun could not shoot something on the other side of a tall ice ridge. Because of all the new and marvelous objects the tribe now had, Allan became something of a hero to everyone, and was considered a very important member of the family. And because he was young and strong and the tribe was short of young men, he became one of their leaders. After all, he had helped to bring them much good fortune.

And yet, not everyone was happy with Allan. Some of the hunters, especially Intuk, did not think too highly of him. Oh, it was true that Allan had helped to find many wonderful new things for the tribe, and his magic was very strong or he would not have been able to tame a polar bear — those things were true Intuk admitted to the others. But it was also true that any ten year old could read tracks that were a mystery to Allan, could smell walrus long before Allan could, could see much further, and even hear better than Allan. As far as Intuk was concerned, Allan was just another mouth to feed, and a mouth that would eat far more than it could find for the tribe.

Still Allan was happy enough with his life. Except for one thing. No one had any idea where the whaling ships could be found. In fact, no member of the tribe had ever been on board a whaling vessel, and no member of the tribe seemed to want to visit one. Every time Allan brought up the subject of whaling ships, people acted afraid and someone soon began to talk of other things. And yet Allan was confident that one day someone would bring word that a whaling ship was upon the sea.

18

The summer came and went. Anxious to get home, Allan often asked about the whaling ships. He wanted the hunters to be sure and tell him if they ever saw such a ship. He himself often went to the edge of the open sea, hoping to spot one of the whalers, but he was always disappointed.

In the meantime Allan accompanied the hunters in their search for food. One day he helped in the killing of a polar bear. Intuk and Krickvik and Ireek and Ootah had gone out on the ice. As they were halted in one particular spot, looking for the breathing holes of seals, the dogs began to set up a terrible racket. They had obviously gotten the scent of something. Intuk jumped up on top of the sled and examined the ice that stretched away in front of him.

"Nanook!" he shouted, jumping down from

the sled. He went to unleash the dogs but the animals were so excited that they got all tangled up in each other's traces. Intuk did not wait to unravel them but quickly drew his knife and slashed the sealskin reins, setting each dog free. When the last of the six dogs went bounding off over the ice, the hunters got the other sled and team ready and took off in pursuit of the free-running dogs. The dogs of the second sled were just as excited about the chase, and the men had a hard time keeping up with them.

Meanwhile, somewhere ahead on the ice, the dogs had caught up with the bear. The hunters could hear the constant hysterical barking that meant the dogs had encircled their prey. And they soon came on evidence that the dogs were not having it all their own way. A dark brown bundle of fur on the trail proved to be one of the dogs. The bear had broken the animal's neck with a slash of its paw.

The hunters could now see the dogs, running in circles around the bear. Every once in a while a dog would rush in and try to bite the polar bear but the larger animal would easily withstand the rush. The bear had absolutely no fear of the smaller animals. As far as the bear was concerned, the dogs were just a nuisance blocking his way.

The sled came hissing up to the scene and

Intuk yelled at Allan to take charge of the dogs and sled. It was all Allan could do to keep the dogs under control. Meanwhile the four hunters had drawn their weapons from the sled. Intuk, who had first spotted the bear, was the first to approach. To him was given the honor of first strike.

Intuk held his lance at the ready and carefully edged closer and closer, waiting for the right moment. A dog made a rush and the bear reared on its hind legs. Intuk ran forward and threw the lance with all his might. The weapon struck home but the bear angrily pawed at the handle until the lance worked loose. Blood began pumping from the wound but the bear ignored the spreading red stain on his fur, dropped to all fours, and charged Intuk. Instantly the dogs attacked and forced the bear to halt.

The other three hunters were ready and one by one they advanced as close as they could to the bear before hurling their weapons. By the time the last hunter had made his thrust, the bear was sitting down with three lances in his body. Intuk now took the killing spear from the sled and advanced to within a few feet of the animal. Then rapidly, so fast that the eye could hardly follow his arm movements, Intuk stabbed the animal's chest with the point of the spear three times. One of the stabs pierced the animal's heart. Blood rushed from that fearful mouth, and it was all over.

Soon they had the animal cleaned, skinned, and loaded on the sled. It was a happy group of hunters who made their way back to camp. One polar bear could keep the whole tribe in meat for weeks. Allan was to take part in several bear hunts after that one and take his turn, along with the other hunters, in hurling the spear.

The tribe moved around quite a bit during the summer months. They made two week-long camps at a lake where low stone walls had been built to capture Arctic char coming in from the ocean to spawn. The hunters guided the fish into a large shallow pool, and then closed the entrance with rocks once the fish were all inside. Then they waded in with fish spears and stabbed downward every time a fish was spotted. Soon the ground around the pool was piled high with the gleaming bodies of large fish. Everyone ate fish until they could hold no more. The rest of the fish were gutted and hung on lines to dry. They would be used in the winter, food for the dogs as well as people.

Another special camp was made for a week while the hunters went out in their kayaks every day to a particular small island to hunt walrus. Every day a walrus was harpooned and brought back to shore to add to the tribe's supply of food. Walrus tusks were highly prized by the hunters, for they made excellent sled runners and the tip of a walrus tusk made a strong, hard point for a harpoon.

For one two-week period all the hunters went inland after caribou. They stalked these deerlike animals with a bow and arrow. Allan accompanied the hunters, although he was not much help to them. He did not know how to use the bow and arrow and he was not very good at stalking. In fact the hunters thought so little of Allan's abilities that they would not even trust him with one of their bows. Allan was determined to learn, however, and borrowed one of the children's bows to practice with. When it seemed as though he would never learn to use the weapon, when his arrows flew every which way except where he was aiming, Allan would think of Bunty Duff. "The master was right," he would scold himself. "You're a stupid clod, without brains enough to cover a sixpence." And once he said that, he would get very angry at the master and decide it was the master who was stupid and not Allan. And some day Allan would go back to Aberdeen and prove it to old Bunty. Some day he would go back and make the master eat his words. And then Allan would go back to practicing on the bow and arrow.

Eventually he became a fairly good shot with the weapon and was able to go out on his own and sometimes bring back a snow hare, or a goose or duck or some other water bird.

During the winter months, when the sea was frozen over, the men lived mainly on seal meat. They went out on the ice almost every day, looking for the rounded small snow domes that meant the breathing hole of a seal. Then a hunter would crouch motionless over the hole, for hours and even a whole day sometimes, his harpoon at the ready waiting for a seal to come to the hole to breathe. As soon as the seal poked his head up through the ice, the hunter struck with his harpoon. The shaft of the harpoon would fall off, but the spear point, attached to a rope, would be lodged inside the animal's body. Eventually the seal would tire and the hunter would "fish" the animal back to the hole and up on the ice. Seals used many holes for breathing and might not come to a particular hole in the ice for days. They had extremely sharp hearing and could sense the slightest movement on top of the ice, which was why it was important for the hunter to remain absolutely still.

Although Allan often tried, he was never able to kill a seal at a breathing hole. He was not patient enough and simply could not stand still for hours the way Intuk or Ootah or Krickvik could.

There was another way of hunting seals, and that was possible in the spring when the sea ice began to break up and the seals no longer had to use breathing holes. The animals would come up through a crack, or an open lead of water, heave themselves out, and bask on the ice. At the slightest hint of danger they would slide right back into the water. When the seals were basking, or lying on the ice, the hunters would stalk them by pretending to be a seal. A hunter would lie on his side on the ice, with one hand slightly raised to imitate a seal's flipper. As long as the seal had his head down, the hunter would wriggle closer, an inch or two at a time. When the seal looked up the hunter would freeze in position and pretend to be another seal.

It usually took hours but the hunter would finally work his way closer and closer until he was so near that he could reach out and touch the animal. When the hunter got that close, he stabbed with the harpoon and hung on to the rope.

Allan was no good at this kind of hunting either. He simply did not have the patience to lie on the ice for hours at a stretch, pretending to be a seal.

Allan found himself in a strange position in the tribe. He knew that with certain kinds of hunting he would only hold the hunters back if he went along. He never forgot one late summer afternoon when a flight of geese came in low over their tents and landed on the waters of the bay. Ootah and Ireek got their bows and arrows and started for the beach. Allan followed them, with a bow and case of arrows that he borrowed from one of the older children. While still a good distance from the beach, both hunters got down on their bellies and started to squirm forward. Allan followed their example but Ootah waved him back. It was plain that Ootah did not want him along and thought that Allan would frighten the birds through his clumsiness.

Angry, Allan went back to the camp and got his fowling piece. He loaded it and started for the beach. He would show them that with his own weapon he was just as good a hunter as anyone else in camp. And he wouldn't have to crawl on his belly either.

He marched ahead of the two hunters and as he was crossing the shingled beach, the geese rose from the water. Confidently Allan raised his weapon and fired.

And missed. Not a single goose altered the rhythm of its wing flaps and soon the dozen birds were a small black arrow flying out over the water.

Ootah and Ireek said nothing, but it was plain that they were disgusted with Allan. Many days later Ireek pointed out that the best Allan could do with his fowling piece was to shoot one bird. After one shot, the rest of the birds would take to the air. On the other hand, the silent arrows might find their marks in three or four plump bodies before the other geese grew alarmed and took flight. The wounded birds, pierced by arrows, would stay afloat until a kayak rounded them up. Feeling very stupid, Allan was careful, from then on, to do exactly what any of the hunters told him to do.

One task that Allan loved was to search the shores of the sea for driftwood, a job that the women usually did. Wood was a very valuable item for the whole camp. Straight pieces could be used to make harpoon handles, or lance shafts, or worked to make the runners or cross slats of a sled. Long curved pieces could be used in making the frame of a summer tent, although whale ribs were also used for that purpose. Wood was so precious, in fact, that it was never burned or thrown away. Even tiny leftover pieces were saved, to be carved into toys for the children: dolls for the little girls and play tools and weapons for the boys.

When he searched for wood, Allan was usually accompanied by Panoo, Ireek's young sister. Panoo was only sixteen and quite beautiful. She had her brother's blue eyes and long straight black hair. She often presented Allan with little presents, usually articles of clothing she had made for him: a pair of waterproof sealskin boots or a double pair of caribou pants or a caribou jacket with a deep warm hood. Allan also went with Panoo to gather seabird eggs and they would spend hours together hunting for the nests of seagulls.

But the main reason Allan wanted to look for firewood was that it gave him an excuse to search the sea for sails of a whaling ship. He still daydreamed of his home in Aberdeen, of his girlfriend Nancy, and sometimes he grew so homesick that he would have welcomed seeing even his old enemy, Bunty Duff.

When Allan could, of course, he hunted with the men. When the hunters would not take him along, he stayed behind in the camp and helped the women, or talked to old Herard, who no longer had the strength to go out and hunt. Allan often played with the children and he taught them a few English words like *snow, ice, cold, Nancy,* and *Aberdeen.* The children were quick to use the English words, whereas the adults would soon give up and say it was impossible for them to pronounce the strange sounds.

And from the children Allan found it easier to learn the tribe's language. They would say a word endlessly until he could repeat it correctly. The adults, on the other hand, would become uncomfortable when Allan tried to speak their language. They felt that it was shameful for Allan not to be able to talk as well as a four-year-old child, and they would lapse into silence rather than cause him any more embarrassment. Nor would they correct him when he made a mistake. It was not considered polite to correct anyone. But the children would howl with glee when Allan made a mistake, and would quickly sing out the correct word or pronunciation.

Sometimes, to please Panoo or the children, Allan would take Nancy for a "Sunday stroll." Arm in arm the two of them would parade back and forth in front of the tents, Nancy waddling along, wrinkling her nose, and sneezing her head off. In the meantime Allan would be walking with his head held high, his belly pushed out, and a very stuck-up look on his face. The difference between his dignified walk and Nancy's comic waddle would have everyone in camp holding their sides with laughter.

As summer passed and winter drew near, Nancy began to act strangely. Sometimes she would moan and whimper for hours. Sometimes she would leave the camp a little ways, and then look out over the ice and snow as though she were expecting someone to come for her. One night she woke up Allan with her moans and cries. He checked to see if there was anything wrong with her. Sometimes ice built up between the soft pads of her paws and this would cause her pain. But her paws were clean. She kept on whimpering and licking his hands and finally Allan made her leave the tent and go outside. Then he went back to sleep and forgot about her. Toward morning he woke up and heard her whimpering. She wanted to come back inside. He shouted at her to be quiet and the whimpering ceased and he went back to sleep.

In the morning she was missing. Allan and Ireek and Ootah began to track her. They followed her for many miles until the tracks came to the open waters of a large inland bay. The bay was dotted with islands, the party did not have kayaks along, and it was agreed to give up the chase. Even with kayaks, they could search the many islands in the bay for months and never find her.

At first Allan was unhappy over the loss of Nancy. She had been such a faithful companion for so long that he had begun to consider her as another human being. But he knew that one day he would leave the tribe and he certainly could not take Nancy on board a whaling ship. If he left her behind with the others it was possible, even likely, that they would kill her during one of those hungry periods when the caribou were absent, when seals could not be caught and even the fish were not to be found in their usual places. Though Allan knew in his heart that Nancy's return to her own kind was all for the best, he never stopped hoping that one day she would return to him. And for a long time after she left, every time he woke in the middle of the night, he would think of that early morning he shouted out to her to stop whimpering. It saddened him to realize that she had probably been trying to say good-bye and he had been too stupid to realize what was wrong with her. It particularly saddened him to recall that his last words to her were angry ones. A thousand times he wished that he could take those angry words back again.

And a thousand times he looked out over the empty wastes, straining his eyes in the hope that he would spot that lovable familiar figure somewhere out there on the ice.

19

And so Allan stayed on with his friends. The seasons passed and he slowly grew more skilled in hunting and fishing, in the customs and ways of the tribe. He learned to speak the language well enough so that everyone understood him. Now that he no longer had Nancy to look after, he moved in with Ireek and his wife Lefa and Lefa's mother, Niapik. Also staying with Ireek was Herard, who was the grandfather of Ireek and Krickvik.

Allan loved Ireek and his family. Perhaps because Ireek was Allan's age he did not seem to be as strict and reserved as Ootah and Intuk, who were mature hunters well over thirty years of age. None of the members of the tribe kept track of their ages so Allan did not know how old anyone was. He guessed though that Herard was over seventy. Herard knew the history of the tribe back for many hundreds of years. Allan liked nothing better, during a long winter storm when everyone was stuck inside their igloos, than to lie on the caribou skins of the sleeping bench and listen to the soothing singsong voice of Herard. Herard could go on for hours in that same soothing chant. At first Allan only recognized a word here and there, but after living with Ireek for some time he realized that Herard's singsong chant was the complete history of the tribe. He realized too that when Herard died, Ireek would be the one to chant the tribe's history so that everyone would remember where they had come from and what adventures had befallen them. And although Ireek gave no sign that he was learning the history by heart, he had heard it so often that he knew the legend word by word without even realizing that he had it memorized.

There was one phrase in the legend that kept occurring again and again and that was the sentence, "But we have now lost the knowledge of those things." One day Allan listened more carefully than usual to Herard's chant, especially the parts that were followed by the sentence, "But we have now lost the knowledge of those things."

When Herard finally finished the legend, Lefa handed the old man a bowl of caribou soup. Allan watched Herard and carefully examined his features: the full flowing white beard, the round, pale blue eyes, the high forehead and cheekbones, the pointed chin. Were the beard trimmed a little, Herard could be a Scottish minister or businessman or judge. And then everything fell into place for Allan. "But you're all descended from the Vikings!" Allan cried.

Herard smiled. The word *Viking* meant nothing to him.

"The pointed ships that could hold the whole tribe, they were the Viking longships," Allan went on. "The long knives that you don't know how to make anymore, they were Viking broadswords. The island that you started out from was Iceland or Greenland!"

But Herard, still smiling, shook his head. The words *Iceland* and *Greenland* meant nothing to him. Allan realized that all the evidence was in the long song that Herard chanted. The "white woolly dogs" were sheep, the heavy horned caribou that gave milk every day were cattle, the big stone igloo was a Viking church, and the land of the igloo roof was glacier-capped Greenland. There was even an explanation of why the Greenland Vikings had disappeared from their two large settlements, as Herard's legend told of bands of hungry polar bears that swept down, winter after winter, and scattered his people. Allan was sure that he was living with a tribe of people who were descended from the Greenland Vikings.

And Herard's story solved a lot of other puzzles for Allan. He now understood the early form of Christianity practiced by the tribe. They had not been recently converted at all, but had held on to their Christian beliefs for many centuries. It was only natural that some of those beliefs would have changed over the years, would have become more simple and primitive.

And the song also explained why the tribe had very little to do with other Eskimos. They knew they were different from the Eskimos, and the Eskimo tribes they encountered knew it also, so that there was little mixture between the two peoples. In fact, in all the time Allan stayed with them, he only knew of one meeting with Eskimos, and he had not been present at the time.

Summer came again, and passed, and came once more. Often Allan feared that he would never leave the Arctic, he was becoming so used to the Eskimo way of life. His memories of Aberdeen grew dimmer and dimmer. The strangest thing of all was that he had trouble remembering Nancy's face. Sometimes he would sit for hours, trying to make a picture of that face suddenly appear in his brain. And yet he could recall his mother's face quite easily, or the faces of his sisters, or even the pinched-in, tight-lipped face of Master Duff. But it was Nancy's face he wanted to recall and when he couldn't it made him very unhappy and depressed.

Sometimes, to keep up his spirits, he imagined what his homecoming would be like. He would walk up Princess Street to Maclean's Drapery Shop. For a moment or two he would stand outside, looking through the window. Then he would spot her, standing behind the counter where the rolls of different cloth were sold. She would be rolling white muslin out from a bolt, measuring three feet at a time from the yardstick nailed to the counter.

He would watch her for several moments, then walk into the shop and go back to her counter. He would stand for a moment while she swiftly scissored through the muslin and folded the material. Then she would look up to see a tall, blonde-bearded man she had never seen before.

"May I have a penny's worth of velvet ribbon?" he would ask. She would go to the ribbon shelf and measure him his velvet. Something vaguely familiar about him would bother her, something about his eyes.

"And a penny's worth of red satin ribbon," he would say when she laid the velvet in front of him.

And now she would be thinking of her first love, that boy who used to spend so much time in the shop, buying ribbons as an excuse, her Velvet Lad who never came home from the sea.

And when the satin ribbon was laid in front of him, he would ask for a penny's worth of green silk ribbon. Sometimes it was at this point that she finally recognized him and cried out his name, as though she were seeing a ghost. But sometimes Allan would let the mystery drag out a little more and his next request would be for yet another penny's worth of ribbon as a present for his sister. At the mention of his sister, Nancy would finally realize who he was.

Yes, he knew such daydreaming was silly, but it helped to pass the time and keep up his spirits. And sometimes he would imagine a meeting with Bunty Duff. He would catch the master by the throat and shake him and ask, "How much brains does it take to live all alone on an iceberg for two years? How much brains does it take to live with Eskimos and learn their language and their way of life? In contempt he would fling the master away from him. "There's more to life than what you'll find in a classroom," would be his final crushing remark.

As the years went by, Allan had many strange experiences with the tribe. He went through some hungry periods when game failed to show up and everyone picked through the gravel on the beaches for seaweed, or scraped moss off the rocks, or went through the heather on their hands and knees looking for berries.

Indeed one early spring, before the fish came back and the walrus returned, when there were no seals to be found, the tribe was forced to kill and eat all but four of their dogs. On another occasion Allan and Ireek took a sled and half a dozen dogs on a simple three day trip to pick up some dead seals from a food cache. The trip turned out to be a disaster. Bears or wolverines had discovered the food supply and eaten all the seal meat. There was one blizzard after another. On the return trip, their food ran out, and they were forced to kill the weakest dog for meat. Every other day another dog had to be killed to feed the two hunters and the remaining dogs. Finally the last dog was killed and eaten, while the two men were in an igloo, snowbound by yet another storm. They began to take apart the sled which, except for the two wooden runners, was made of walrus and caribou bone. They broke the slats and sled handles into little pieces and made bone soup of them. When the sled had been all broken up and eaten, they started in on the dogs' sealskin harness and ate every one of the sealskin lines and traces. They even ate the long dog whip, which was made of plaited walrus hide. When the harness was all eaten, they began to cut small pieces off their clothing and spent hours chewing on the dried caribou skin of their jackets.

When they finally made it back to camp, they were but shadows of their former selves. Everyone else had given them up for dead. And yet a week later they were well and fit, and Ireek was eager to go seal hunting once again. But on that one trip they had eaten their six dogs, the dogs' harness, the sled, their caribou-skin blankets, a snow knife made from a caribou shoulder blade, and even some of their own clothing. It was a lesson in survival that Allan never forgot.

One late summer Allan was in camp with the women and children when the returning kayaks of Intuk, Ootah, and Krickvik were spotted on the water. The three hunters had gone off on a two-day trip to see if any caribou could be found.

Everyone ran down to meet the returning hunters and Allan helped carry the kayaks up on the beach. Then he asked Intuk the question he always asked, the answer to which was always no.

"Did you see any big ships?"

Intuk's twisted face turned away from Allan and he began to yell at some children who were dragging a caribou-skin blanket on the beach. "Pick that up! Put it away on a pole somewhere. You want the dogs to eat it?" Behind the tents were a couple of platforms on top of poles where the dog harness and extra food were kept so that the dogs could not get at it.

Allan looked at Ootah and asked, "Were there any big ships?"

Ootah did not answer and busied himself with something in the kayak.

"Krickvik!" Allan called.

But Krickvik was already marching up the beach in the direction of the camp.

Allan was very puzzled by the conduct of the hunters. He had never known any members of the tribe to tell a lie, though they might exaggerate something in telling a funny story. But he had long noticed that rather than tell a lie, they would simply say nothing, or refuse to answer a question. Was it possible that they had spotted a whaling ship and did not want to tell him?

He was walking towards Ireek's tent when half a dozen children suddenly swarmed all around him. "Allan Gordon, Allan Gordon," they chanted. "Take us back up the mountain. Pili has thrown out her bed and needs new heather!"

They clung to his arms and jacket and led him back up the slope behind the camp. Sometimes the women in the tribe would decide that the pile of heather that was used as a mattress during the summer was too full of bugs. Suddenly a woman would be seen dragging all the heather out of a tent and within an hour or so all the women would be throwing out their old mattresses. Then the women and Allan and the children, and even old Herard, would gather armfuls of fresh heather and bring them inside the tents and lay them down on the gravel until the bed part of each tent had a nice clean sweet-smelling heather mattress again.

High up on the slope above the camp, while the children ran around looking for clumps of the tiny heather, Allan sat down on a large stone and thought about the returning hunters. Could it be possible that they had seen a whaleship and were not going to tell him? If so, he would wait until everyone was asleep and then steal a kayak. He knew roughly in what direction the hunters had gone in their search for caribou. He would try and retrace their route and hope to run across a sailing ship.

Just before everyone was ready to come down from the slope with their armfuls of heather, Allan noticed half a dozen hunters come out of Ootah's tent. There was Ireek and Krickvik and Intuk and Ootah and even old Herard. Something about the way they came out of the tent made Allan think they were having an important meeting. And if they had such a meeting without him, then it meant that he was the subject of their conversation. Had it anything to do with the returning hunters? It was all very strange, and he would have to talk to Ireek.

For one thing, Allan could not understand why no whaleships had been spotted by the members of the tribe. All during the whaling season, one or more hunters would be out on the sea in their kayaks, looking for game. Had something happened to end the whaling voyages? Had the whales disappeared from Arctic waters? Had a great war broken out in Europe, a war among the half dozen nations that sent out whaling ships? Allan knew that the men of the tribe did not like to talk about the whaling ships. Had something happened to cause this fear? Could it be that some members of the tribe once had dealings with men from a whaling ship, a meeting that had turned out badly for the hunters? So badly that they now avoided all contact with the ships, avoided even the mention of them?

Allan hurried down the slope and brought his heather into Pili's tent. The children followed him, and for half an hour he played with the youngsters in the piled-up heather, wrestling with them, pretending that he was a bear and they were hunters, or he was a walrus trying to overturn their kayaks. But finally Pili got annoyed with their play and chased everyone outside.

Allan made his way to Ireek's tent. He ducked his head and entered the outer, lighter part of the tent where Lefa was sewing some fox-fur mittens. Allan smiled at her and went through and into the inner section.

Ireek lay on the sleeping platform.

"So, brother, what does Intuk say about the caribou?" Allan asked.

"There were no signs of caribou."

"And so, they saw nothing strange?"

Ireek ignored the question. He sat up, took out his short sled knife, and started to carve a small piece of wood. Soon the head of a bear began to take shape.

Allan waited. Ireek would speak when he was ready.

Finally Ireek asked, "You still want to go back to your own land?"

"Yes."

"You do not like it with us?"

"I want to see my own people again."

"You will not take a wife from among us?"

"No. There is a woman at home who is promised to me," Allan said.

"Yes." Ireek understood that. In the tribe marriages were sometimes arranged many years in advance and children as young as four or five were often promised to each other in marriage by their parents.

"They saw large boats," Ireek said.

"Boats? Sailing ships? How many?"

Ireek put up one hand and spread his fingers.

"Five sailing ships?" Allan repeated. Part of a whaling fleet on its way home! And even if he missed the five ships, surely there would be others. But he had to find out what route the hunters took, where they had spotted the ships.

"Some of us did not want to tell you about the ships," Ireek said. "You know you are like a brother to me and our family will miss you. We do not want to see you leave. Others said you might guide us to another ship trapped in the ice. They said that was your spirit gift, as Intuk's gift is hunting and Ootah's is sealing and Inusklik's is curing sicknes. Some said that you would take a woman from the tribe and start a family. As you know we are short of men and we have too many women."

"But you decided to tell me?"

"Yes. Herard and Intuk said you should leave and go back to your own people. Intuk said that some day soon you would learn how to find the ships by yourself and then you would bring your people back to punish us for keeping you here."

"No, I would not do that. But Intuk has never liked me."

"Intuk is a great hunter," Ireek said. "But because of his face he thinks that people do not like him, so he does not like people."

Allan thought of the fortuneteller. Was Intuk his dark enemy with the scarred face? "How did his face get so scarred?" Allan asked.

"It happened one winter when he was a baby and there were hungry times. His mother lay on the sleeping bench in her igloo. She was so weak from hunger she could hardly move. Intuk was inside the hood of her jacket. A starving dog came into the igloo, dragged Intuk out of the jacket, and began to eat him. His mother spilled hot oil from the lamp on the dog's eyes but Intuk was already bitten and missing half a cheek."

"So that is why Intuk beats the dogs so much?"

"Yes. You know too that Herard said that the sea spirit would keep the seals away from us if we made you stay."

"Then I can leave?" Allan cried out in sudden wonder.

"Yes. They are making ready a kayak for you."

20

Intuk drew the route with a stick on the sands
of the beach. He showed several small bays, a
string of offshore islands, then a great headland jutting into the sea. Allan committed the
map to memory. The hunters had no maps or
charts, nor could they write. But they had excellent memories and were capable of tracing
a coastline with their knives on a flat piece of
bone, or drawing it from memory on sand or
gravel.

Enough dried fish and caribou and seal
meat to last a week was stowed into the front
of the kayak. Everyone, it seemed, brought
Allan a present; a piece of clothing or a special item of food. They crowded around him
on the beach and old Herard hobbled down to
lay his hands on Allan's head and bless him.
And although Herard could not read, Allan
gave him his Bible as a present because he
knew how much the old man would treasure
a history of his faith.

The only one who was missing was Panoo. Pili said that Panoo had run off and was hiding back in the heather because she could not bear to see Allan go away.

Even Intuk seemed sorry to see Allan leave. "If you do not find your ships, then come back to us," Intuk said.

"I will," Allan promised.

Then he gave Ireek his fowling piece, and hugged him and Lefa his wife, and climbed into the canoe. His paddle flashed as he drove the kayak out from shore. As long as he was in sight, the people on the beach kept waving to him. Finally though, he rounded a point of land and even the tents were no longer visible. By now Allan had learned how to handle one of the tribe's skin canoes and he made slow but steady progress, following the shoreline to the south.

It was strange, but he now felt homesick for his friends. He had grown to love their simple ways and quiet dignity. Indeed he halfway hoped that he would not find a whaling ship and be forced to return to the village. Think of the welcome he would get and the feast that would be made ready.

Because it was late summer, with almost continuous daylight, Allan could travel all day and most of the night if he wanted to. Once in a while though he would land, prop the canoe on edge to provide shelter from the wind, and cut himself a few slices of seal meat and grab a couple of hours sleep. As soon as he woke up, he would return to the sea again. There was still plenty of loose ice on the water but Allan was able to maneuver his kayak through the floes without any trouble.

On his third day out, Allan came to the great headland jutting out from shore. He landed his canoe, climbed to the top of the hill, and looked to the south. A beautiful sight met his eyes! There, out on the open sea, were two whaleships, both with full sail and drawing away from him. He hurried back down to the foot of the cliff, launched his kayak and gave chase. He rounded the bluff and now saw, that no matter how hard he paddled, the ships were too far away and moving too swiftly to over-take.

For a while he rested in the canoe, very very tired and very unhappy that he had missed the ships. Then he turned the kayak around and headed back to shore.

Dragging the canoe well up on the beach, he examined his store of food. He unwrapped the caribou-skin bundles that contained meat and a dozen dried fish. He had enough, if he ate sparingly, for another four or five days, maybe even a week. He would camp there on top of the bluff and keep an eye on the open water to the north. There was still a very good chance that more whaling ships would be coming through. And like the ships already gone past, they would probably sail within sight of the bluff. The high bluff was a good landmark, and unless a ship came through while Allan happened to be taking a nap, he was almost sure to spot anything heading for the point.

Making sure that his canoe was well above the highwater mark, Allan unloaded half his food to be carried to the top of the bluff. The rest of the food he left inside the upturned kayak. If he needed more food, he could come back for it later. On top of the bluff he stored the meat and fish under a layer of rocks.

He scraped out a hollow on the windward side of his rock pile and settled down to wait. He would camp there until his supply of food ran out. Then he could always go hungry for the three or four days that it would take him to return to the tribe. His only problem was water. However, he knew that some of the ice floes were made of old sea ice from which the salt had already been melted out. All he had to do was paddle out and locate an old floe.

He looked out over the water. As far to the north as he could see, the surface was studded with ice floes. It would not be long now, he thought, until those floes came together to form rafts and islands and continents of ice that would completely cover whatever open sea was left.

Because he had nothing to do, he decided to make a stone landmark, a tower of rocks and stones that could be seen from far out to sea. The Eskimos often made such towers to guide them to certain spots on land when later they were far out on the frozen ice, or in kayaks on the sea. Fortunately there were plenty of rocks on top of the bluff and he spent five or six hours building his tower. When it was finished it stood about ten feet tall. Then Allan took the canoe paddle, tied a caribou wrapping skin to the blade, and stuck the paddle on top of the tower. Finally he stood back to admire his handiwork, his signal for help. Now if he were sleeping and a ship drew close, his makeshift flag might be enough to draw a landing party.

As he waited he thought how foolish he had been to give away his fowling piece. He might have been able to shoot some birds, ptarmigan or seagulls, or even use the shotgun to signal with. On the other hand, it would have been hard to keep the gunpowder dry in the kayak, and, anyway, Ireek needed the gun more than he did. It was just as well.

He had brought along his carving knife. He needed it to cut pieces off the frozen fish and seal meat. After years of use the knife looked nothing like the knife Allan had picked up on the *Anne Forbes*. The blade had been ground away so much that it was only half the length that it used to be. In fact Allan had to be very careful when using the knife. The metal was now so thin that the blade might easily snap in two.

As the hours passed and Allan waited in his shelter, he grew more and more lonely. It was the first time since the *Anne Forbes* had gone down that he found himself completely alone. Always before, there had been either the members of the tribe or Nancy for company. He wondered now where his pet bear was, and supposed that she had already raised several families since leaving him. He still missed her and he knew that he would miss his Viking descendant friends. He had grown to love them all, even Intuk. Often he had spent weeks at a stretch with a half a dozen others confined to a tiny igloo or tent, with hardly room to turn around. Such confinement either made for deep hatreds or long-lasting friendships, and he had been very lucky in that only friendships had grown out of his experiences. In fact, after he and Ireek had almost starved to death on that one trip, they had come to love each other, and Ireek often called Allan his brother.

As he waited on the bluff, Allan was tempted

several times to give up his search and return to the tribe. He had been happy with those simple and kind friends of his. And anyone who remembered him back in Aberdeen would remember him only as a young lad who had been lost at sea. Even his mother and sisters would have gotten over his disappearance by now. And Nancy? It was when he thought of Nancy that he knew he had to go back. He had promised her that he would return, that nothing would happen to him, and he intended to keep that promise.

One thing his long years in the Arctic had taught Allan and that was patience. Where another, less-experienced man, might have paddled up and down the shoreline looking for ships, perhaps losing himself or dying of exhaustion, Allan calmly waited on the bluff, knowing that if any ships were still around they would eventually pass his lookout point.

He did not have long to wait. The next day he spotted sails to the north, what appeared to be a three-masted bark. He grabbed his paddle, came running down the bluff and launched his canoe. He set a course that would cut across the vessel's path, paddled out, and waited. Several hours later the whaling ship bore down on him, its deck crowded with curious sailors.

Allan rested his paddle across the kayak and

shouted up, "I'm a shipwreck, a castaway. Can I come on board?"

None of the sailors made any offer to help, and the captain, standing on the quarterdeck, angrily waved Allan off, making signals for the kayak to return to shore. Allan was stunned and for a moment unable to think. As the ship slid past he reached out and touched the wooden side of the vessel. He had touched a ship bound for Europe, a ship that could carry him back to Scotland, and yet no one on the ship would even talk to him!

For several moments the kayak bounced around in the larger vessel's wake. Then Allan drove his small canoe out of the rough water and rested for a moment as he stared after the whaleship. He found it hard to believe what was happening. They had actually no intention of taking him on board!

21

As Allan watched the whaler draw away from
him, he felt an overpowering anger. What
was wrong with them? Could they not tell he
needed help?

Savagely he dug the end of the paddle into
the sea. His arms a blur of motion, he sent the
kayak skimming over the water in pursuit of
the larger ship. Half an hour later he caught
up with it. He noticed a rope trailing down the
vessel's side, caught the end of it, and let the
larger ship tow him along.

Four or five faces stared down at him. Re-
calling his first meeting with the Eskimos,
Allan shouted up, "In the name of Jesus
Christ, take me on board!"

The captain joined the half dozen sailors at
the rail. He was Dutch and had, for the past
hour, seen the Eskimo canoe on the water, obviously waiting for his ship. The canoe was
handled so expertly, as Allan maneuvered to

keep his position among the ice floes, that the captain was sure that the person in the frail craft had to be an Eskimo. Then too Allan was dressed in furs and skins, typical Eskimo clothing. The captain was anxious to get back to Holland with his catch, to get out of the Greenland waters before the ice caught him. He did not want an Eskimo on board. He did not want to waste an hour or two to find out that all the Eskimo wanted was to trade a mangy fox fur for some tea or tobacco. He was so sure that he had an Eskimo to deal with, that even if Allan had spoken in Dutch, the captain probably would not have recognized his own language.

But when Allan repeated his cry for help the third time, the captain recognized the name *Jesus Christ* and some of the English words. Like most seagoing men of that time, he knew some useful phrases in half a dozen languages in addition to his own. For a long moment the captain stared down at Allan and Allan stared up at him. Silently Allan prayed that God would make the captain understand. The captain shouted something and Allan held his breath. A dark bundle of some kind was being tossed out over the rail. Were they throwing garbage at him? The bundle stretched out and Allan recognized a rope ladder. He let out a sob and grabbed the end of the ladder. Then he stepped up on the bottom rung and tied the trailing rope to his kayak. A minute later he was standing on board the Dutch whaler *Briel*, homeward bound for Holland.

The captain invited Allan to his cabin and called for the ship's carpenter, who spoke English, to interpret for him. As Allan moved away from the rail, a flash of white on the shore caught his eye. He turned back and saw a polar bear scramble up a short dark slope and melt away into the heather. Though the bear was too far away for Allan to make out more than the animal's general size and shape, he called softly out over the water, "Good-bye, Nancy."

An hour later, in the captain's cabin, Allan learned to his astonishment that he was one week short of having spent seven full years in the Arctic. In turn the captain found it hard to believe Allan's story and questioned him again and again. Indeed, in the following weeks, the ship's carpenter was constantly asking Allan to answer the questions of the captain or members of the crew.

In return for passage home, Allan gave his kayak to the captain. He also traded all his Eskimo clothing to members of the crew for regular European clothes. Three weeks later the *Briel* halted briefly off the eastern coast of

Scotland to transfer Allan to a small coasting vessel. The coaster eventually took Allan back to Aberdeen. When he arrived in his home port, he stepped off the trading ship and the only souvenir he had of his seven years in the Arctic was his poor, worn-down carving knife that had helped kill two polar bears.

The day Allan landed in Aberdeen he left the quays and made his way to Princess Street. It was an unusual afternoon for that part of Scotland, a warm sun with not a trace of cloud in the sky. As he walked up Princess Street he wondered if Nancy would recognize him. He had changed, had grown a good three inches, and added thirty pounds to his weight. He was also wearing a full blonde beard and hair down to his shoulders.

He passed by Craigie's Tailoring Establishment and thought with special fondness of that skinny twelve-year-old lad who used to work there. Finally he stood on the wooden sidewalk outside MacLean's Drapery Shop. He lowered his head and peered in the window. There was a young girl standing behind the counter where Nancy used to stand.

He went inside and nodded to the elderly woman who was seated at the high desk. Then he walked down the aisle and stopped in front of the girl. He wanted to ask her for a penny's worth of black velvet ribbon, but he had no money in his pocket. Indeed he had not handled any money in over seven years.

"May I help you sir?" the girl asked with a smile.

"Yes." Allan found it difficult to ask the question for he was still not used to speaking English again. "There was a girl worked here seven years ago, Nancy Campion. Does she still work here?"

"Oh no, sir, Nancy left a couple of years ago. She lives in Edinburgh now."

"In Edinburgh?" Allan repeated.

"Yes, sir. She married a solicitor's clerk from there."

Allan turned away and left the shop. He should have expected that, he told himself. Why would she wait seven years and her not knowing if he was alive or dead? And yet he did not expect that she would be married, and somehow he felt hurt that she had not waited for him.

Lost in his memories, his feet automatically took him long the well-known streets and alleyways of his boyhood. By coincidence he walked past the ironmonger's shop where he had left his gift of grapes for Nancy so many years before. He remembered his promise to bring her back some grapes from Vinland and smiled. Minutes later a small elderly man, coming out of a bakery shop, almost bumped into him.

The man muttered something and hurried away. Allan stopped to stare after him. It was Master Duff, and he had not changed a bit. There was still that thin nose and tight pinched lips and deep-set suspicious eyes. For a moment Allan was tempted to run after the master, to stop him and demand an apology for those remarks of so many years before.

But instead he laughed. What difference did it make? He did not feel hatred anymore; it was all gone. It was funny, he told himself, but two things had kept him alive all those years in the Arctic, his hatred of Bunty Duff and his love of Nancy Campion. And now that he was back home he discovered that he did not need that love, nor that hatred either. They had already served their purpose. In fact he didn't need anyone's good or bad opinion of him. He knew exactly who he was. He was Allan Gordon, twenty-four years old and strong as an ox, smart enough to have lived through experiences that would have killed a dozen others. He knew who he was and what he was capable of, what he was made of, and that was a gift far greater than the treasure that the old fortuneteller had said he would bring back from his voyage.

He would go home now to his mother and sisters and talk for half the night and finally climb the ladder to the loft above the kitchen and sleep in his old bed and feel just like a twelve-year-old again — for one night at least. Because in the morning there was a whole new world waiting for him, and somewhere a new Nancy.

And as he walked through the pleasant sunshine he raised his hand and touched the invisible gold ring in his ear, then smoothed the feathers of the imaginary parrot that sat on his left shoulder. The Velvet Lad was gone for good, but "Iceberg" Gordon had finally come home.

22

What you have read is more or less the story that Allan Gordon told when he came back to Aberdeen after being away for seven years. Do you believe the story? Many of Allan's friends and neighbors did not. Who could believe that a teen-ager would be able to kill, with his knife, not one but two full-grown polar bears? Who could believe that someone like Allan, with no experience in training animals, could tame a polar bear so that she would hunt and fish for him?

Old whaling sailors were full of scorn. They said the winter ice in the Arctic moved around so much, was so affected by underlying ocean currents, by tidal changes, by the force of winds, that the *Anne Forbes* would surely have been crushed to pieces that first winter. Anyway, icebergs always drifted to the south and warmer waters where they soon melted. Many of these sailors had seen hundreds of such icebergs off the coast of Greenland, all drifting south. Then too, drifting icebergs had a tendency to roll over every month or so, as the waters ate away at the undersea part of the berg and the upper part became top heavy. Also icebergs continually "calve" off smaller icebergs from their edges. Old whaling hands claimed that the ledge on which the *Anne Forbes* rested would surely, in the course of two years, have broken off to become a growler.

Other sailors claimed that Allan could not have survived so long on his iceberg without fresh fruit and vegetables. He would surely have died of scurvy.

Most incredible of all, however, was Allan's claim to have lived for years with a tribe of Norse Greenlanders, descendants of the Vikings. These Greenland Vikings had all disappeared around the year 1500, whether killed by disease or wiped out by Eskimos, no one knew. In 1721, some thirty-five years before the *Anne Forbes* went down, Hans Egede, a noted Danish missionary and explorer had sailed for Greenland to look for the lost colony of Vikings. He found nothing but ruins where the Vikings once lived, and although he fully explored their two main settlements, he found not a single descendant of the estimated five thousand Vikings who had been living in

Greenland in 1250. So much for Allan's claim to have lived with Vikings.

And so Allan's story was at first flatly denied by many, especially those who went on whaling voyages. However, there were some facts that had to be believed. Allan had been away for seven years and the *Anne Forbes* disappeared without a trace some seven years before. It was known that Allan had sailed on that ship. There was that horrible scar on his arm and shoulder that certainly looked as though some large animal had taken a bite out of him. The old whaling men, however, were still unconvinced. After all, the *Anne Forbes*, beset by foul weather, might have put in at the Orkney or Shetland or Faroe islands, or even Iceland, all places that were on the direct run to the whaling grounds. There Allan could have jumped ship and later signed on another vessel bound for a European port. He could even have remained on land those seven years, working on an Icelandic farm or sheepherding in the Shetlands. Jumping ship was not an uncommon practice among whaling hands.

And Allan's scar? Well there are many men with scars on their bodies from accidents, from being caught in machinery, or falling onto something sharp and jagged. Allan's scar proved nothing. In fact his story was so full of holes that it plainly revealed his ignorance of the Arctic seas. Take, for example, that band of polar bears he and Nancy had run into in the dead of winter. Anyone who knew anything about the Arctic knew that polar bears went into hibernation at the first sign of snow. No, Allan had never been shipwrecked on an iceberg, had never tamed a polar bear, had never lived with Viking descendants, although he certainly knew how to tell a tale, that much the old whaling hands were prepared to give him.

Nevertheless, some years after Allan's return to Aberdeen, the story of his polar adventures became generally known throughout his native country. Many people argued about Allan and his story, some believing it to be true and others claiming that it was all a pack of lies. Strangely enough, one man who believed Allan's story was Master Bunty Duff, Allan's old schoolteacher. In fact Master Duff spent some time writing down the whole of Allan's adventures. Then one day, early in the 1800s, James Hogg, a well-known Scottish writer and a friend of Scotland's national poet, Robbie Burns, got hold of Master Duff's account of Allan's adventures. The story so impressed Hogg that he included "The Surpassing Adventures of Allan Gordon" in a book of his published in 1836 and called *Tales and Sketches of the Ettrick Shepherd*.

With the passage of time, as more and more facts about the Arctic became known, more and more of Allan's story began to seem possible, and more and more people believed that Allan just might be telling the truth.

While it was true, for example, that many icebergs drift south to where a northern arm of the Gulf Stream melts them away, by no means do all icebergs end up this way. Icebergs have been known to drift south along the east coast of Greenland, reach the tip of that huge island, and there get forced by tides into the northflowing current that moves up the west Greenland coast. It is even possible for an iceberg to make a complete circle of Greenland, though it would probably take many years to do so.

Nor is it true that all icebergs tumble and turn topsy-turvy every so often. Some icebergs are so huge, several square miles in area and hundreds of feet thick, that their very size prevents them from overturning. Such icebergs, if they do not crack apart, are simply too large and bulky to turn upside down. In fact such floating "ice islands" are now used, from one year to the next, by certain nations as scientific outposts for predicting weather.

Nor was there anything unusual in the *Anne Forbes* being forced up on an underwater ledge of the iceberg. The same thing happened to Captain Kane, an Arctic explorer, in 1853 when his ship, the *Advance,* was forced up the side of an iceberg by currents working against an underwater ramp. Everyone abandoned the vessel but later they managed to get the ship off the berg, only to have it frozen into the sea ice. Kane and his companions lived two years on the imprisoned ship before they were able to get away. They faced terrible hardships; three men died and others were crippled for life before their two-year ordeal was over.

As for killing a huge polar bear with a knife, many Eskimos have been forced to kill such bears with a knife when their spears have not struck a vital part of the animal. Then too, Allan had help in each of his fights. On the first occasion the bear had been jammed in the window frame of the cabin, unable to turn around. The second polar bear had received a full load of shot in the head before Allan jumped in with his knife to finish the animal off.

Tame polar bears may have seemed incredible to the whaling men of Allan's day, but today we know that many polar bears have been tamed. If the ordinary brown bear, a first cousin to the polar bear, can be taught to ride a bicycle, then training a polar bear to catch and bring back fish does not seem all that unusual. Even before Allan's time, men had caught polar bear cubs after killing their mothers, then trained such cubs from infancy. In fact, the practice became such a sport in Iceland in the Middle Ages that the Icelandic authorities passed laws stating that such tame bears were to be considered the same as dogs; that is, the owner was responsible for any damages the animal caused.

While it was generally believed in Allan's time that polar bears hibernated all winter, in actual fact only pregnant females do so. Males and nonbreeding females hunt right through the Arctic winter of constant darkness. Allan's whaling companions could not know this, of course; few had ever lived for a winter in the Arctic. All they had seen were female bears in the spring, coming out of their snow dens, and because of this it was commonly believed that all polar bears holed up for the winter.

To the charge that Allan would have died from scurvy, medical science has pinpointed salt meat as the chief villain of the disease. It is true that fresh fruit and vegetables will prevent scurvy, but large quantities of salted meat seem to hurry the onset of the disease. Allan ate as little salt meat as possible, living mainly on fresh frozen meat and fish. Some Eskimos thrive on such a diet and never see fresh fruit from one year to the next.

The weakest part of Allan's story was his claim to have lived five years with "old Norsemen," or descendants of the Greenland Vikings. The last reported contact with Greenland Vikings had been around the year 1500, a good two hundred years before Allan was shipwrecked. And yet there is no satisfactory explanation as to why a settlement of some five thousand Vikings simple disappeared. Perhaps Herard's story of being overrun by hordes of starving polar bears provides as good an explanation as any for the breakup of the Viking settlements.

Whatever may have happened to these Norse Vikings in Greenland, it is still possible that a small band of them joined forces with a band of Eskimos, intermarried and had children. There are hints in Allan's story that he fell in with such a mixed tribe. Very few, if any, Eskimos of that time were Christian, yet Allan's tribe knew the name of Christ and practiced some Christian beliefs. These beliefs may have come down from the Viking half of the family. The leader of the tribe, Herard, had a long white beard. Few Eskimos grow beards and when they do such beards are short and scanty.

While dog teams, skin canoes, and the larger open boats (kayaks and umiaks) are typical of Eskimo life, hardly typical is the larger number of females, women and children, in the tribe. There were, according to Allan's story, thirty-one women and ten men. He also mentions seven children, only two of whom were boys. Now most Eskimo tribes, until very recent times, were careful to keep the sexes even in number. It was a fairly common practice, for example, to allow girl infants to die. They were simply put out in the snow until they froze to death. This may seem cruel to us, but the Eskimos knew that the women would eventually outnumber the men if all the infant girls were allowed to live. The life of the Eskimo male was so dangerous, in comparison with the female, that he died or was killed far more often than the female. Eskimos knew that if a family contained too many women, the fewer number of males would simply not be able to find and kill enough food to provide for everyone.

Yet there were twenty-one more women than men in Allan's tribe, which means that they did not follow the usual Eskimo practices of keeping the number of females roughly the same as the number of males. Perhaps it was because they were Christians and such acts were forbidden by the Christian religion. Or was it because such practices were never allowed by their Viking ancestors? In any event, the overbalance between women and men probably led to the disappearance of the tribe through starvation not too many years after Allan left them.

Allan's story has three possibilities. Either it is true, it is false, or some of it is true and some of it is false. It may well be that Allan was wrecked on an iceberg but picked up a short time later by a Danish or Dutch whaling ship. He may have spent the next seven years working in Holland or Denmark, so that there was no Nancy, no fight with the large polar bear on the ice, no five years with the Viking descendants. He may have invented all those stories in the hope that people would treat him as a hero when he finally came home.

And yet the story has the ring of truth about it. And would Allan, making up such a story, have invented so many little things that were widely believed to be false by the people of his time — details and facts of Arctic life that later turned out to be true?

Whether the story is true or false is perhaps not important. Certainly the events were not impossible. We know that other men have survived equally incredible dangers and hardships in the Arctic. What is important is that we want to believe that the story is true. We want to believe that man is capable of overcoming the dangers that Allan overcame. What young man has not imagined himself as a castaway on an island, face to face with hostile natives? With only his two hands, his brain, his determination and courage to see him through? What young man has not dreamed of training a powerful wild animal to come to his call? As one writer said of Allan's story, "Well if it didn't really happen, it should have."

Some of Allan Gordon's descendants came to America in the last century. So if your name is Gordon, you may be descended from the Iceberg Hermit.

point

Other books you will enjoy, about real kids like you!

- ☐ MZ42599-4 **The Adventures of Ulysses** Bernard Evslin — $4.50
- ☐ MZ42771-7 **Blitzcat** Robert Westall — $4.50
- ☐ MZ43715-1 **Escape from Warsaw** Ian Serraillier — $4.99
- ☐ MZ40943-3 **Fallen Angels** Walter Dean Myers — $4.99
- ☐ MZ44479-4 **Flight #116 Is Down** Caroline B. Cooney — $4.50
- ☐ MZ45898-1 **The Glory Field** Walter Dean Myers — $4.99
- ☐ MZ44110-8 **The Greek Gods** Evslin and Hoopes — $3.99
- ☐ MZ43136-6 **Missing Since Monday** Ann M. Martin — $3.99
- ☐ MZ42792-X **My Brother Sam Is Dead** Collier and Collier — $4.50
- ☐ MZ44651-7 **Sarah Bishop** Scott O'Dell — $4.50
- ☐ MZ42412-2 **Somewhere in the Darkness** Walter Dean Myers — $4.50
- ☐ MZ45680-6 **The Stranger** Caroline B. Cooney — $4.50
- ☐ MZ43486-1 **Sweetgrass** Jan Hudson — $3.99
- ☐ MZ48475-3 **Talking to Dragons** Patricia C. Wrede — $4.50
- ☐ MZ47478-2 **Twins** Caroline B. Cooney — $4.50
- ☐ MZ43412-8 **Wolf by the Ears** Ann Rinaldi — $4.99

Watch for new titles coming soon!
Available wherever you buy books, or use this order form.

- -

Scholastic Inc., P.O. Box 7502, 2931 E. McCarty Street, Jefferson City, MO 65102

Please send me the books I have checked above. I am enclosing $_____ (please add $2.00 to cover shipping and handling). Send check or money order — no cash or C.O.Ds please.

Name_____**Birthday**_____

Address_____

City_____**State/Zip**_____

Please allow four to six weeks for delivery. Offer good in the U.S.A. only. Sorry, mail orders are not available to residents of Canada. Prices subject to change. PNT298